THE FIRST LADY & THE WRITER, PROVINCETOWN 1961

A Novella

Brenda Pizzo

The First Lady & The Writer, Provincetown 1961 by Brenda Pizzo is a work of historical fiction. Any resemblance to persons living or dead, places, or incidents is a product of the imagination of the author or used fictitiously.

Copyright © 2020 by Brenda Pizzo

All rights reserved

Library of Congress Cataloging-in-Publication Data

Title of Work: The First Lady & The Writer, Provincetown 1961

ISBN9798218564544

Cover design and illustration by Brenda Pizzo

Copyright © Brenda Pizzo 2021 Second Printing 2024

The First Lady & The Writer, Provincetown 1961

Table of Contents

FOREWORD	6
If the Shoe Fits	7
Pink Carnation	17
Don't Sew in the Label	32
Red Carpet	43
The Mona Lisa	58
Scrub Pines & Weathered Shingles	72
A View with a Room	79
Salems not Gauloises	96
The House with the Columns	108
Dressed to the Nines	121
Khrushchev's Puppy	127
Defying Gravity	137
Mufflers & Elevators	156

Blue Hair & Flappers	*172*
Queen of Sheba	*184*
Tomorrow	*196*
~Author's Note~	*199*
~Acknowledgements~	*204*

FOREWORD

A small item that once appeared in a Provincetown newspaper said that on August 31, 1961, the famous author, Gore Vidal, invited First Lady, Jackie Bouvier Kennedy, who later became Jackie Kennedy Onassis, to spend the afternoon and evening with him in Provincetown, Massachusetts on Cape Cod.

This was no small thing because at that time, it bears mentioning, Jackie Kennedy was the most famous woman on earth. The newspaper item mentioned that the two ate dinner at a restaurant, saw a George Bernard Shaw play in the local theater and pointedly noted that at the end of the evening, they were refused entry into a private drinking club.

The idea of Jackie palling around Provincetown with Gore for a day, unnoticed, had great appeal. What was it like for her to act like a tourist for a day? When I decided to write a short novel using them as my subjects, I researched what was going on in the world and in their lives during that period in history to bring enrich their conversations.

The following story is a work of historical fiction about real people, who in their time, were larger than life.

IF THE SHOE FITS

November 1963

When the news bulletin was broadcast across the world, Gore Vidal was in a cinema in Rome. Eight months previously, before the shots rang out in Dallas and stopped the world in its tracks, Vidal had already been iced out.

Gore boarded the first flight out to Washington to attend the funeral of JFK, as he was known to the world by just his initials. Soon after arriving, he found that a place for him in the church was not possible. There were others more important, and it seemed, that crushingly, anyone other than him even a lowly bureaucrat ranked a seat. This hurt him terribly. On the street, in the chill, and anonymously in the crowd, he watched outside the Capitol, as the coffin was brought slowly and deliberately down the steps. However, hurt as he may have felt, this was no time for pettiness. Still, he knew it was Bobby who had his hand in the affront, but he had only himself to blame.

After the assassination, it must be noted, Jackie Kennedy received more than two million letters of condolence. The first forty thousand came to the White House within three days. But a letter from Gore Vidal, her once friend and confidant, was not among them. Nor was there any sort of contact, not even a phone call. It should not have come as a surprise. Eight months previously, Gore had written a scathing magazine article that appeared in Esquire *Magazine* in the 1963 March issue. In the article, he laid out the reasons why he believed Bobby (RFK) should not be successor after JFK's second term. Because Bobby, saw the world only from his black and white lens, Vidal reasoned Bobby was too rigid and too autocratic to make a good and effecting president. In Bobby's world, there were no grays.

Gore was not entirely sure if he was partly motivated in writing the piece for *Esquire* by an incident that had taken place his last evening at the White House in the fall of 1961. Nevertheless, even if there had not been a blow up, he would have arrived at the same conclusion regardless. The magazine article caused not only outrage within the family but also a sensation in the political sphere. Ranks closed in around Bobby and Jackie fell in-line with the rest of them. Family loyalty was everything. There would never be another chance for his cherished friendship with her to bloom again. Even so, the world spinning out of control and all doors firmly shut to him did not stop him from paying his last respects. Jack was a man he had much admired, had shared a wicked sense of humor, including a like-mindedness for living life unconventionally by his own rules and had called a friend. Returning to Rome, Gore vowed he would never put himself in a vulnerable position again. He had reached the end of his rope, which was shorter now than it had ever been. He knew his worth. Regret was for the past and he was only going forward.

October 24, 1961

It was at a party at the White House that the trouble began. It was an unseasonably balmy night in Washington. Like a switch by November the evening temperature would turn brisk as soon as the calendar page turned. The guests were turned out in evening attire. They were an attractive sophisticated bunch from the world of politics, as well as some upper echelons of high society. Hollywood was also represented, thanks to actor, Peter Lawford, husband to Patricia, the President's sister. Lawford had many actor friends, who in turn had become their friends and added to the many intriguing people found at their private White House soirées. Those not included found themselves on the outside. If you were not stimulating, attractive, or vital enough to be a part of this new vibrant White House Washington scene, and you lived in Washington, yours was a sorry predicament.

Gore was wearing handsomely tailored evening clothes he had bought from a shop in Rome. It was almost impossible to live in Rome, which he did part-time with his partner, Howard, and not be influenced by the smart style of Italians beautifully turned out. The shop windows were full of fine clothing. The Italians oozed sex appeal and were living embodiments of style. Men wanted to be Marcello Mastroianni and women wanted to be with him. Gore had seen Mastroianni twice in the streets of Rome. Once in Piazza del Popolo as he was heading toward Via del Babuino, an over coat suavely draped over his shoulders and sporting dark Ray-Bans that disguised his identity, or perhaps Mastroianni only imagined they did.

Another time, he saw Mastroianni getting into a taxi. Romans, a smooth cosmopolitan lot, never appeared too eager for anything. If

Mastroianni was spotted, no one was willing to be the first to point at him or notice. Perhaps, Sophia Loren, out and about, may have garnered a different result but Gore was never able to affirm his theory as Loren did not frequent public spaces.

Howard had encouraged Gore to purchase patent leather tuxedo slippers. The handmade shoes fit like a glove and were patterned from meticulous measurements. The shoemaker kept the pattern on file in perpetuity. If Gore desired, he could write from America and request an entirely different style shoe and it could be made and shipped without having to step into the shop. After some persuasion, it was an extravagance he afforded himself. With invitations to the White House, evening dress had become part of his life.

However, he was no stranger to midnight dinners at New York's El Morocco or hosting his own dinner parties in Rome at two favorites, Ristorante Nino, located near the Spanish Steps or the old-world, Piperno's, in business since 1860, located in the Jewish ghetto and best known for delicious fried artichokes. For these evenings in Rome, an open collar dress shirt, smart slacks and a jacket was all that was required.

The women were always fancier, pulling out all the stops. Close-cropped hair that framed their faces, a la Gina Lollobrigida, seemed to be all the rage. Their lips colored in various shades of bold red lipstick, their dresses body hugging, and wearing gold hoop earrings along with sexy high heeled strap sandals, they sent a message of expectation. Gore wondered how the women navigated cobblestone streets in those shoes. Perhaps it was one of the reasons, Italian women relied on a man's arm so vehemently.

In Venice, he liked Harry's Bar; in Paris he had a few bistros and brassieres that he frequented, but that depended on which neighborhood he stayed. He thought the French, especially the women, un-usually attached to their dogs. It was common to see dogs in restaurants sitting under the table of their owner. If only the French would learn to pick up after their dogs, especially in places like Nice, where it became second nature to vigilantly dodge out of necessity. In London, he stayed with various friends in either their townhouses or country retreats.

Gore was accustomed to living in the world, not just a small piece of it. His group of friends spanned the globe. He loved the stimulation that cities provide but he never turned down the opportunity to explore a hideaway or an exotic little-known locale. When Paul Bowles invited him to

Tangier, he did not hesitate to accept. He even considered moving there. Approaching forty and still handsome, he began to feel it was time he dressed the part.

He was pleasantly enjoying himself outside with a Cognac and a Cuban cigar. These evenings could go either way, fascinating and fun, or a colossal bore. It was impolite when an invitation came to ask who else was coming? It was Jack himself who had offered him the cigar. Outside, there was a smallish group sitting around chatting, enjoying a breeze. Inside, people were dancing the samba. It was late. After all, the parties began at ten and generally went into the wee hours of the morning.

"So, Gore," Jack began, "tell me, when in Rome, what's popular cocktail-wise? What do the Italians like to drink?"

"The Negroni, of course, *still*...since 1919. But you know Italians, 1919 is like yesterday to them!" Gore chuckled. "The drink's name, Negroni, comes from Count Camilo Negroni. It was the Count who asked his bartender to strengthen his favorite cocktail, oddly enough a popular drink called an *Americano*, by replacing the soda water instead with gin."

"No kidding," Jack remarked, "there was an

13

Italian drink called an Americano in 1919?" This fact tickled him. He crossed one leg over his knee and leaned back grinning. Just then, Jackie came outside a bit flushed from dancing. Gore rose and offered his chair.

"Was that David Niven, I saw you dancing with?" Gore asked.

"Yes," she replied seating herself and smiling at him.

Turning, she then engaged in conversation with the person to her left. It is blur just who was outside at that moment. Gore remembered leaning over Jackie, resting a hand on her bare shoulder to whisper in her ear some fun gossip he'd overheard. They were laughing together when seemingly out of nowhere, Jack's brother, Bobby, physically removed Gore's hand from Jackie's shoulder.

"Just what do you think you're doing?" Gore asked, his response bordering on outrage.

"I don't like your filthy hand on her," Bobby said menacingly.

"I beg your pardon, just who do you think you are?" With that Gore gave Bobby a shove. Bobby shoved back.

Now they were several feet from the others and the argument was intensifying.

"I'm her brother-in-law and you're nothing but a filthy fairy."

"I'm no fairy Bobby and you know it!" Gore said, a powerful anger rising. Towering over him by three inches made him appear even larger compared with Bobby's slight frame.

"Don't hold back Bobby, 'fairy' isn't really the word you had in mind, is it?" He was poking Bobby in the chest now.

"What exactly is your beef?"

"You know perfectly well, Vidal. What *you* do is unnatural. It's against nature. It's filthy and I don't want those hands touching my brother's wife."

"I don't ascribe to *your* rules," Gore shot back, "The Catholic Church has no bearing on my life, and it certainly doesn't dictate every aspect of yours!"

"What's that supposed to mean, you son of a bitch?" Bobby was in Gore's face just inches away.

Teeth clenched, Gore countered, "Did you tell *your* wife what went on at the Lawford's Malibu beach house? I was there the night Marilyn met you." Gore's eyes widened, "Even God himself couldn't save you from *her*."

Instead of punching Bobby in the face which would have given him immense satisfaction, Gore

15

grabbed his dinner jacket from the back of the chair knowing that he had landed a blow, albeit metaphorically. For him, the evening was over. Gore left the White House.

Even after the altercation, Gore was still on good terms with Jackie and Jack. Though the incident swirled in Washington gossip circles, ever level-headed Jack considered what happened a private matter. Gore continued to write letters to Jackie from Rome, and she returned the correspondence with personal handwritten letters to him from Washington. They even occasionally spoke on the telephone.

Gore took responsibility for what had happened next. It was his pointed article "The Best Man 1968" published in *Esquire* in March of 1963 that broke the friendship.

Jackie never spoke to him again.

Pink Carnation

August 31, 1961

The telephone rang twice before the call was answered. The phone light blinked, signaling that the call was for her if she wished to take it.

"Hello?"

"Jackie, it's Gore. The weather looks clear, are we still on?"

"I'm looking forward to it. Does four-thirty work?"

That's fine. Why don't you come to my hotel? I want to show you, my view."

"I trust that's not a euphemism," Jackie demurred.

"Certainly not," Gore replied, laughing. "Room 13."

"Thirteen? That number doesn't worry you?" Jackie teased.

"I'm not superstitious." Gore answered chuckling.

"Okay. I'll be the one wearing a pink

carnation."

She hung up the receiver on her bedside table. The small clock face displayed quarter past eight. As she slipped down in her bed under the covers, she stretched out her whole body extending her arms over her head, her hands clasped against the tufted headboard covered in gray blue linen. She was thinking about what she would wear and how much fun she was going to have spending the afternoon and into the evening with Gore.

Gore Vidal was a celebrated and prolific essayist and writer. A cultivated person, with patrician manners and a sharp wit. He was also highly opinionated, and Jackie liked that. Shrinking violets were not her milieu. She knew Gore ascribed to Alice Roosevelt Longworth's approach to people, which was, "if you haven't got anything nice to say about anybody, sit next to me."

Still, Gore was much more than a mere gossip. His style was prone to an off-handed quip, shooting off a real zinger when he felt the situation warranted it. For instance, he could not bear the thought or the sight of the author, Truman Capote. He once quipped that if a Brussels sprout could speak, it would sound like Capote. As anyone would expect, the zinger did not win any points of admiration from Mr. Capote. Close in age, they had both won notoriety early in their careers which manifested a competition between the two that morphed into rivalry.

There was a soft breeze. The sheers fluttered lightly in all five windows, each framed by chintz drapes printed with a motif of pink cabbage roses on a white background. The air smelled sweet as morning air does. Sunlight ricocheted from the water nearby, reflected on the ceiling and sparkled like diamonds. On the painted powder blue bureau, were a collection of family photographs in silver frames. Among them was a favorite of herself at age three standing with her father, a tall and attractive man who cut a dashing figure. Another photograph, captured at just the right moment shows Lee, her baby sister, who four years younger, is just a year-old to Jackie's age five. The two little girls are sitting on a beach in bathing suits; Jackie wears a white bathing cap and Lee wears a wild expression on her face and is so excited about something her legs extend stiffly in front of her. A timelier picture is one of Jack, looking adoringly at baby Caroline in her bassinet as she lay on her stomach lifting her baby head to smile broadly up at him.

On the painted white walls, other family

photographs hung depicting a time span from childhood memories to the present and mingled with a display of some of her favorite personally executed watercolors.

Jackie sat up in bed as she spied the doorknob turn this way and that. The door cracked open just enough for a small blonde head to pop in. It was three-year-old Caroline.

"I see you," Jackie smiled.

"I see you too, Mommy." With that the little girl entered the pristine white room filled with sun light and chintz and climbed up onto the bed to give her mother a hug.

She looked up, "I'm hungry."

Jackie squeezed her close and kissed her on the top of her head.

"Me too. Let's get some eggs."

Jackie threw off the white bed covers and stood on one of the three powder blue area rugs around her bed. At five feet seven inches, she was above average height. Proud of her twenty-five-inch waist, she tasted dessert but rarely ate it. She had a swimmer's build with broad shoulders and slim hips. She could have easily gone braless if it were acceptable. It was not. A dark brunette with wide-set brown eyes, she had a sculpted nose and a generous pouty mouth.

She opened her closet door and pulled out a yellow sleeveless shift dress from a quilted hanger. She slipped out of a short nightie and placed it on a small bedroom chair that was covered in the same fabric as her linen headboard. She did not bother with putting on shoes as she enjoyed going barefoot in the beach house, especially in summer. Her feet were uncharacteristically large for her height at size ten. She was in good company as she and Audrey Hepburn could swap shoes.

She smoothed her hair with her fingers as she picked up the phone and pressed the button to ring the Secret Service trailer located on the grounds.

"Good morning, Agent Hill speaking."

"Mr. Hill, if we want to arrive at four-thirty this afternoon, what time do you suggest we leave Hyannis Port?"

"I'll have the car ready and waiting for you at three o'clock."

"Thank you." She hung up and replaced the phone in its cradle.

"Caroline let's get you changed for breakfast."

They walked down a hallway that was papered with a green ivy trellis design, into Caroline's room. Jackie opened the top drawer of a

21

tall dresser and selected a pair of plain white cotton underpants for Caroline along with a yellow short-sleeved jersey. In the second drawer she found the pair of denim overalls she had in mind. Caroline unbuttoned her pajama top by herself. It was white and printed with little pink bows and pink piping. Jackie helped her with the rest.

"Mommy, do I need to put on shoes for breakfast?" Caroline asked.

"Not if you don't want to," Jackie smiled. "Let's get the baby." Caroline grinned at both remarks.

John, nine months old, lay in his crib, babbling happily to himself. He had been fed his seven-a.m. bottle which was clearly marked on the chart near his crib. Jackie lifted him and checked to see if his diaper was dry. "How is our little John today? Did you have a good sleep? Did you, did you?"

She nuzzled him and rubbed her nose against his. The baby reacted with a squeal and a wide smile.

"Mommy, can I hold him?"

"Not now, Caroline. Maybe later. Let's get our breakfast, shall we?"

Jackie positioned little John against her body letting him wrap his arms about her neck. She kissed his baby cheek, soft as a peony blossom, and the crook of his neck drinking in the fragrance of the curls on his head. His warm, sweaty head smelled sweet.

As they walked down the hallway, Jackie said, "Now Caroline, please remember, this is important. You are not allowed to take John out of his crib or to hold him without supervision. He may look like a doll, but he is not a doll, but a real baby who could be easily hurt."

"I know, Mommy, I only talk to him in his crib, I don't try to take him out," said Caroline earnestly as she held the banister and walked behind her mother down the bare wood stairs.

Jackie turned to look at Caroline who made eye contact, "Thank you, Caroline. You know Mommy is counting on you."

A warm breeze circulated in the kitchen. When the house was built for them, Jackie requested plenty of windows and chose unfussy knotty pine cupboards, a sink of stainless-steel, and cobalt blue colored counters. The house had hardwood floors throughout but, in the kitchen, she had red linoleum. The kitchen was recently papered in a yellow and white gingham pattern and had half curtains in the same gingham. The curtains were spread to allow the breeze to come in.

Upon entering the kitchen, Jackie greeted her cook who was standing at the ready. Rita, a woman in her mid-fifties of slim build and medium height had a local accent and thick dark wavy naturally streaked, salt and pepper hair. Her short hair framed her face, crowning at least two-inches high, with a widow's peak, that sat squarely in the middle of her forehead. Without a lot of fuss, she looked fresh in a starched light blue sleeveless dress and navy-blue espadrilles. She occupied herself, reading the morning paper by the window in sun dappled light. She was pouring a second cup of coffee from the percolator and stubbing out a Winston cigarette when Jackie came into the kitchen.

Rita lived just a stone's throw on nearby Irving Avenue, a street that bordered the Compound. This was convenient, as she could arrive for work at a moment's notice, return to her own house during the day at intervals and return to make supper for the family or cook dinner for a party. A wedding band was her only adornment to freshly washed hands with fingernails that were never painted she felt for obvious reasons. She kept a dish towel handily on one shoulder. It was an easy walk from her house to the Kennedy's summer residence. She had a comfortable relationship with the family generally and with the First Lady in particular. However, in no uncertain terms did she boast or brag to anyone, even when she was the lucky recipient of a hand-me-down dress, blouse, or skirt. Jackie had been raised to be frugal. Never one to throw away anything she felt could be useful to someone else; she always had a recipient in mind. "Rita, do you think this dress is something you could use?" Jackie would ask before bestowing an article of clothing she no longer felt an attachment. Rita was only too happy to be on the receiving end.

"Good morning, Mrs. Kennedy," Rita looked up and folded the paper. "And how are you today, little Miss Caroline looking all spiffy and ready for the day?"

"Good," Caroline nodded and smiled shyly.

"Very well, thank you," Jackie gently corrected.

Caroline repeated her mother's phrasing.

"That's very nice to hear," Rita encouraged the little girl. Jackie lifted the highchair tray and settled the baby into his seat. She lowered the chair's tray table while Caroline handed John a spoon which he banged on the wooded tray top making only himself happy with the noise.

"Coffee, Ma'am?" asked Rita. She placed the morning paper and a small pitcher of milk on the table.

"Yes, thanks. Can anyone resist coffee in the morning?" Jackie asked with a smile. "Anything happening in the *Globe*?"

"The first Peace Corps volunteers are off to Ghana," Rita announced as she reached up and took a cup and saucer from the cupboard. As she poured the coffee she continued, "A good picture of the President with them at the White House."

Rita placed the cup of coffee at Jackie's place on the table and opened the newspaper to show her. "He sure looks happy."

"Look, Caroline, there's your Daddy in the newspaper," Jackie pointed to the picture.

Caroline perked up and asked, "Who are those people with Daddy?"

"Good question, Caroline," Jackie answered, "these young people will bring medicine to children who live very far away in a country called, Ghana."

"Why?" asked Caroline.

"The children need vaccinations so they won't get sick," Jackie explained and added, "Another reason they are going is so our country can be friends with their country."

The explanation made Caroline smiled.

It was Gore Vidal who came up with the idea for The Peace Corps. He thought there should be more than just the armed services as a way for young people to serve their country and he presented the idea to Jack. Only Gore's original idea was for the Corps to be just a national program. JFK expanded it when India and African countries reached out and asked for help. JFK determined the program would make allies and influence diplomacy at the same time, giving young people an invaluable life experience. He floated the idea in a speech at a university commencement and immediately afterwards a thousand students signed up and joined.

"Rita, may we please have some scrambled eggs? I'll make the toast. Do we have any grape jelly?"

"Oh yes, there's a jar in the fridge and more in the pantry." Rita pronounced the word, more, as if it had two syllables instead of just one and ended the word with a short "a" sound. Like most of the locals, Rita had a "Boston" accent. "More" became, moe-ah!

Continuing she added helpfully, "If that jar in the fridge is getting low, we have two jars in the pantry," not pronouncing her "r", "jar" became "jah."

Jackie opened the bread box and took out a

27

loaf of bakery bread. "Caroline look, oatmeal bread, your favorite!"

"Goody," remarked Caroline. Delighted, she clapped her hands.

Jackie popped two slices in the toaster and got the butter dish from the counter. Grabbing a box of Cheerios, she dipped a half cup measurement into the box and poured the contents into a hard plastic bowl. She set the bowl down on the highchair tray table. The baby delighted in dumping the bowl, picking up a Cheerio he brought it to his mouth. His aim was improving.

"Mommy, John's making a mess!" exclaimed an indignant Caroline.

"Yes, he certainly is, isn't he?" Jackie took a bottle from the cupboard and filled it with chilled apple juice. Closing the refrigerator door, she said to Caroline, "It's what babies do."

John took the bottle from her and tilted his head back against the chair as he drank.

"Good boy, John," Jackie smiled broadly, "How big you are, drinking your bottle all by yourself."

Jackie opened a cupboard door and grabbed two yellow, cloth napkins. She asked Caroline to put the napkins by their breakfast plates. Caroline was only too happy to oblige. She climbed up on her chair, better to reach the table and perched on her knees carefully placed a napkin on the placemat next to each plate. Jackie was unconcerned whether the child placed the napkin on the correct side of the plate. At the Cape, Jackie liked breakfast casual. The table could have been set, but she liked the idea of letting Caroline help with small tasks. Life was not magic. She felt Caroline should understand that helping was a joint effort. It was also her commitment to her children to raise them as normally as possible.

"Mrs. Kennedy, did I mention my niece is getting married in October in Washington?" Rita began, "We were wondering if you could recommend a nice hotel?"

Jackie sipped her coffee and looking up at Rita answered, "How lovely. Washington is so beautiful that time of year. There's no need for a hotel, Rita, we have plenty of guest rooms at the White House."

"Oh, I'm so embarrassed, I didn't mean..."

Jackie waved her hand, "Nonsense, Rita. It will be our pleasure. Imagine how excited Caroline will be to see you there. It will thrill her to introduce you to Macaroni, her pony. Tack on a few more days so you and Ned can take in the sights, there's so much to see."

Satisfied Jackie added, "There, it's settled."

Rita brought two plates of fluffy scrambled eggs to the table and said, "I can't thank you enough. I can't wait to tell Ned!"

Jackie smiled, "Don't thank me yet, Rita, the mansion is in a restoration quagmire, but I'll make sure you have a nice room."

"Mommy, do you know why?" Caroline piped up claiming some attention for herself.

Jackie smiled, "What is it?"

Caroline, making eye contact, shifted in her chair, a look of mischief in her eyes. "Mommy, do you know why the cookie went to the doctor?"

"Hmmm," Jackie frowned playfully, "I'm not sure. Why *did* the cookie go to the doctor?"

Caroline touched her index finger to her lips, "Because," she broke out into a smile, "...because it was feeling crummy!" She tried to keep her composure but broke out in a fit of giggles.

Jackie laughed too. "That's a good one. You must tell Daddy that riddle. It's just the sort of joke he likes."

Pleased with herself, Caroline picked up her napkin, unfolded it and placed it in her lap.

As Caroline and Jackie ate their breakfast, Jackie proposed, "Caroline, shall we see what shells we can find on the beach this morning?"

Caroline nodded yes, finishing her juice in one long breathless gulp she placed the glass on the table.

"Move your glass, honey, it's too close to the edge."

Don't Sew in the Label

Wearing a thin white terry cloth robe, Jackie sat at her vanity table with a towel twisted on her head. The painted bench seat that matched the vanity faced the water view. Two milk glass lamps with pink shades flanked the three-way mirror so she could make up in day or evening. She listened to the waves lapping on the beach below. A warm glow of sunlight filled the room. She was enthusiastic to spend a day away from the Compound, to be a tourist, unnoticed and unencumbered. This was not a day of duty but a day free from any responsibility, not that she had many, if any, official summer commitments.

Washington was another matter entirely but even there she was able to control her schedule. Both her mother and her mother-in-law were happy to play hostess to a ladies' tea because most of the time she was not up to it. There was also another she could call upon, Lady Bird Johnson, the Second

Lady, who was southern charm personified and who offered, with heartfelt sincerity, to help Jackie in any way she could. Lady Bird understood only too well the demands on a young mother. Jackie, if she could be faulted, hated small talk and being on display. She made it a rule not to attend dinners of visiting dignitaries or heads of state unless their wives came along. There was only so much time and she preferred to devote as much time as she could with her young children. Today was an exception as she was flexible when the opportunity was something she favored.

She was excited to spend the day with a friend, an almost relation, in Provincetown, a small fishing village that was located at the very tip of Cape Cod. On what was a beautiful Thursday summer day in August, she was hoping to blend in as inconspicuously as possible. When she spoke with Jack earlier in the week and told him her plans, he was more than encouraging and seemed almost envious.

Jack thought that Gore was fun and interesting company. Jack, like Jackie, also liked that Gore had opinions that he was not shy about expressing. Similarly, Gore liked that Jack was ruthlessly confident. On one of their first meetings, they were riding in a limousine together when they were both ushers at Gore's half-sister, Nini's wedding. In the limo, Jack blurted out that he believed Nini would be better off marrying Jack's brother, Teddy. Gore thought it was an impulsive thing to say but then his sister's groom *was* twice her age. Gore, himself, had responded to the groom's invitation to be an usher rather flippantly, when he wrote a response note that he thought marriage was such a disastrous step, he would be only too happy to be a witness to the groom's folly!

Gore's world revolved around ideas. He had an interest in many subjects and could speak on a variety of topics off-the-cuff. When Jack became the president, he conferred with Gore on several issues and took advantage of Gore's modern approach to help him in his quest in shaping ideas for a new generation. Jack was interested in Gore's unique point of view, just as he was interested in what Jackie's thoughts were regarding issues and people. Often, Jack used Jackie as his sounding board. Because she was more intuitive about people than he was, she was a good judge of character and rarely was she wrong about someone. More so now than ever, Jackie's importance grew as Jack absorbed the weight of the office.

Jackie had just turned thirty-two years old. As she peered at her reflection, she began her routine by applying moisturizer to her face and neck. She removed the towel and dried her hair with it removing as much wet as possible. Beginning by combing a section of hair from the top of her head, she rolled her hair around a large roller. She continued the process until all her hair was rolled. Taking the portable hairdryer from its case, she placed the inflatable bonnet connected to a long hose on her head and plugged the cord into an outlet. She set the control to "hot" and turned on the machine. Then, with cigarettes in hand, she moved to a comfortable chair and arranged her legs comfortably on a hassock and settled in to read *French Vogue* for half an hour. She fretted about the humidity. She hoped while she walked the beach town her hair would not triple in size as if it were rice. If only her hair were straight, it would not be so prone to frizzing and such a worrisome concern.

Caroline ran by her mother's room but stopped long enough to say, "Mommy, you look like a Martian from outer space!"

Jackie looked up and smiled, then went back to reading. While flipping through the magazine, a dress by the French couture designer, Hubert de Givenchy caught her eye. It was a cocktail dress with a full skirt that had a *décolleté bateau* neckline that came just below the collar bone. The sleeves were full-length, but the most intriguing feature of the dress was it was backless and decorated with a flat bow at the waist. She did not think she would be able to wear the dress to an official function. She and her designer friend, Oleg Cassini had a devil of a time convincing Jack that strapless gowns were appropriate for official dinners and as classic as the ancient Greeks and Egyptians. Jack relented and Jackie got her way. But this dress *oozed* sex. She convinced herself it was suitable to wear for their intimate White House parties.

Walking over to her writing desk, she opened a drawer and took out scissors. She lay the magazine flat on the desk and cut the dress out of the magazine. Carefully folding the page, she placed it into an envelope and wrote a note in her loopy handwriting, "Tish, please contact House of Givenchy in Paris and ask to have this dress made for me in midnight blue dupioni silk. It is in this month's *French Vogue*. Please ask Mr. Givenchy to send to W.H. and not sew in his label inside the dress. Also, ask him to have evening shoes made in the same fabric. Pointed toe and a three-inch heel seem right. A small evening bag too. He will know just the one. TY -JBK."

She placed the envelope, with other ready-to-go correspondence, on her desk. She would deal with sending it out tomorrow. She addressed another note to Tish with whom she shared a long and storied history.

Letitia Baldrige, known as Tish, was a classmate of hers when they both attended Miss Porter's School, an exclusive preparatory boarding school for girls in Connecticut and Vassar College. Tish now enjoyed the prestigious, if not exhaustively demanding position as Jackie's social secretary. In order, to get to Jackie, one had to go through Tish.

"Tish," Jackie's second note began, "Sometime in October my cook, Rita is coming to Washington to attend her niece's wedding. Would you please have Mr. West get in touch with Rita to learn dates, etcetera? Please tell Mr. West to give her a nice W.H. guestroom and please ask him to work out an itinerary for best sights, The Library of Congress should be among them. TY -JBK."

She folded this second note and placed it in another smaller envelope all on its own and added it to the bigger envelope of correspondence and instructions.

Time up, she removed the dryer bonnet from

her hair and removed the hair rollers. She waited a bit for her hair to cool before combing and sat down at her vanity to make up. With her tanned skin, not much makeup was necessary. Her freckles came out in summer, something in youth that bothered her but now she was used to them. Besides, Jack thought they were cute.

Caroline came into the room breathless from running up the stairs. Her shoelace was untied so her mother retied both with a double-bow knot. Caroline climbed up on the vanity bench and sat beside her mother as she looked intrigued at her own reflection. Jackie smiled at her as they looked at each other in the mirror. Jackie picked up a fat makeup brush and swirled it with some pink blush. She then brushed the apples of each cheek.

Picking up a powder puff, Caroline powdered her tiny nose, quite pleased with herself. Jackie took the makeup brush, and this time gave Caroline's cheeks a pink glow. Caroline studied the result turning her face left then right one eye in the mirror. Opening a tube of frosted pink lipstick Jackie applied a coat. With confidence she finished her look with black eyeliner and mascara. Picking up one of her perfume bottles, a grassy fragrance, she gave herself a spray on her neck and wrists. The transformation was quick.

Caroline asked for some perfume, "Me too, Mommy, me too!"

"Show me your wrists," Jackie suggested. Caroline obliged and Jackie gave them a short spray. Caroline rubbed her wrists together as she had observed and immediately brought them to her nose. She inhaled deeply and smiled. Jackie brushed her hair and invited Caroline to brush her own. Caroline did her best to mimic her mother. Jackie picked up a canister of *Aqua Net* hair spray.

"Cover your eyes and hold your breath. Mommy has to spray her hair."

Obediently, Caroline put her hands to her face and took a deep breath that she held. She listened to the aerosol spray and spread her fingers to peek. The mist fell all around her.

"Coast is clear. You can breathe now."

Jackie removed her robe, underneath she was wearing a matching set of pretty, white lace lingerie, a habit she had picked up while she studied as a coed in Paris. One thing Parisian women insisted upon was attractive matching underwear sets. She stepped into a pair of white Capri pants that zipped up the side. She carefully pulled a fitted, sleeveless blouse in a delicious shade of pink over her head. It buttoned in back, so she left just enough buttons undone to pull the blouse over her head. She easily reached and fastened the top three. Her tan color flat, Italian-made sandals slipped on easily. Her jewelry was simple, a plain gold wedding band, a tank watch with a beige ribbon strap, and two thin gold bangle bracelets.

"You look nice Mommy," Caroline offered. Jackie smiled, bent down and asked Caroline for a kiss. Caroline wrapped her arms around her mother's neck and kissed her cheek. Jackie hugged her back with a gentle squeeze.

"Be a good girl," Jackie said, as Caroline ran off to play with her cousins who were calling for her from downstairs on the first floor. "Uncle Teddy is taking you to get ice cream a little bit later."

"Oh, goody," Caroline called back from the staircase she was carefully descending one step and one leg at a time.

Jackie listened to the uneven rhythm of Caroline's descent. Grabbing a straw summer bag and surveying a final glimpse in the mirror, Jackie also made her way downstairs. Opening the dark green screen door, she emerged from the house.

Along with a beach ball left haphazardly near the steps there was a pail and shovel. A beach station wagon car was parked in the rounded horseshoe shaped driveway. Also close by, in the back, a picnic table sat in the yard on an expanse of green lawn. The yard was surrounded by privet hedges and a white picket fence. A clothesline had Caroline's red bathing suit and two striped beach towels hanging to dry. Nearby, stood similar but not identical white clapboard houses of various sizes but none so big as the main original family dwelling.

The atmosphere in the Compound was chummy and relaxed. Children came and went in each of the houses as if they were their own. No request for a peanut butter and jelly sandwich, a drink of water, milk, or juice was refused. Tonic, which the rest of the country called soda or pop, was reserved for special occasions, such as the children's birthday parties. Fruit bowls overflowed to the brim and cookie jars were never empty, but permission had to be granted before the cover was removed and little hands dipped in. "May I" and "thank you" were phrases all the children learned early and said often. Play times and playmates seemed endless and so did summer on Cape Cod.

The most exciting event on the Compound happened weekly in summer when on Friday afternoons the President's helicopter appeared in the sky and hovered above, just before it landed on the lawn. All the children would come running. The helicopter door opened, the blades still whirling, the engine roaring. There, Uncle Jack appeared in the doorway beaming. The throng of kids greeting him knew to stand back at a safe distance. He would walk out of the chopper clearing the blades and would be surrounded. Grinning from ear to ear, he would greet and speak to each one, as the littlest of them grabbed him about his legs. Caroline would hardly be able to contain her excitement. Jack would slip into the driver's seat of his golf cart that was parked nearby on the lawn and the kids would pile on. He always made sure to put Caroline on his lap. Off they would go across the lawn at a good clip; three kids in front with him, more kids in the back seat, and a few older ones hanging on the back for dear life. It was a sight to behold and an exercise no one tired, no matter how many times it was repeated.

The patriarch of the family, Jack's father, made it a point and a practice to be sitting on his wraparound porch when the helicopter landed. Jack made sure his detail radioed ahead to give his father the heads up.

The screen door clapped shut behind Jackie audibly. She smiled and gave a short wave as she came down the steps.

Red Carpet

Standing by the car was a man in his late twenties of sturdy build. Clint Hill, a Secret Service Agent, was dressed in an open-collar short sleeved-shirt, light-weight cotton trousers and slip-on loafers. He was dressed casually for this outing to better blend in with vacationers and locals. He had taken care to wash and wax the car, vacuumed both the front and back, cleaned the windows from the inside, emptied the ashtrays, filled the tank, checked the oil level, the fan belt, the radiator water level, and the tires.

Special Agent Clint Hill was the man recently promoted in charge of her detail. He took the job seriously. It was both an honor and a privilege, not to mention a huge responsibility. He had guarded presidents previously and, at that time, could not image anything more important than guarding the most powerful man on earth. Somehow, this assignment carried just as much weight.

The very first time he laid eyes on her; she was eight months pregnant. He and his boss had been sent over to the then Senator's Georgetown house to make their introductions to the President-elect and his wife. While they were exchanging pleasantries with the Senator, Jackie came into the room perfectly coiffed in a pretty maternity dress. It was the President-elect himself who introduced them. Hill recalled how the soon- to-be-president called him, Clint. But she did not do that, she called him, Mr. Hill and said how nice it was to meet him. Their meeting was brief. She apologized; she was tired. It was late afternoon and she hoped they could excuse her; it was time for her to rest. The new President shook Hill's hand warmly and told him that it meant a lot to him that he would be taking care of his wife. Pending their approval, Caroline would be assigned her own agent. Of course, Hill understood the gravity of his new position, but hearing it put in such a way underscored the dimension of the responsibility.

That first meeting seemed eons ago. His assignment had not been even a full year, but already so much had happened. JFK was invited to a summit in Vienna that took place in June of 1961. The President decided that Jackie would be a valued asset and with his wife in mind, he took the opportunity to expand the visit to include London and Paris as an added enticement for her. The red carpet was rolled out in all three capitals. What transpired was both fantastic and unprecedented. To say their tour was a success, in Paris especially, would be an understatement of epic proportion.

The queen hosted a private dinner for them with sixty people at Buckingham Palace. At the start of the evening, it was not a little exasperating for the queen to observe her assembled guests exit the reception room en masse to witness JFK and Jackie ascend the staircase, the throng peering over the balcony in both judgement and awe. Jack, while holding Jackie firmly by an elbow, looked up and smiled a seductive beaming grin. Jackie delicately lifted the hem of her gown to reveal evening shoes in matching fabric. As she took the stairs, she was conscientious of her every step. This was not the moment to stumble. Jackie caught Prince Philip's eye. His face was the only one she recognized.

The glamour of the Americans escaped neither Queen Elizabeth nor Prince Philip who witnessed it upon their arrival, the queen, ever reserved, took it in as they entered the room where she remained standing ready to welcome them.

Jack bowed from the neck, while Jackie took the queen's offered gloved hand in her own gloved hand and curtsied. Wanting to be graceful and respectful she had practiced her curtsy in front of a full-length mirror.

"What a pleasure it is to meet, Mr. Kennedy, Mrs. Kennedy. How wonderful that you could make time in your busy schedule for us" the queen chirped, offering a pleasantry in her clipped way of speaking.

"Your Majesty," Jack formally addressed his hostess, the young queen, who at thirty-five years old was in her prime. "It is an honor to meet you and high time we buried the hatchet," Jack said with a wide grin, a twinkle in his eye.

The queen laughed. "Surely, you know FDR and my father managed that."

JFK laughed, throwing his head back, not anticipating such a swift comeback. Elizabeth was quick on her feet. Her first Prime Minister, Mr. Churchill, had taught her well.

Recovering, Jack said, "So this is what they mean by rolling out the red carpet, it is a pleasure to be here."

"Don't think of it." She smiled, "We are happy to have you. We trust, being president is everything you *didn't* imagine?" the queen asked wryly.

"It's not nine-to-five," Jack answered, cocking his head.

"No. What job is?" the queen smiled.

"Nine-to-five jobs," Jack said and laughed.

"Indeed," the queen agreed. "Mrs. Kennedy, I understand you are teaching your daughter to ride horses."

"Yes, your Majesty, Caroline has a pony named Macaroni," Jackie explained.

"Such a charming name for a pony," the queen laughed.

"Yes, I'm afraid that's what happens when you ask a three-year- old what she would like to call her pony." Jackie smiled.

"I am not certain I could do better," the queen remarked making the three of them laugh.

"At the time, I questioned Mrs. Kennedy about the name, wondering if Caroline hadn't misunderstood the question and was answering what she wanted for lunch," Jack said, amusing all of them.

"Ma'am, it is lovely of you to have us like this. Jack and I were so looking forward to meeting you and coming here. I was in London for your coronation, and I wrote a column about it when I worked for a newspaper in Washington," Jackie offered.

Queen Elizabeth brightened, "I remember the day well."

"We all do. How wonderful that it was televised," Jackie said.

For both Elizabeth and Jackie, 1953 was a monumental year. It was the year that Jackie and Jack were married, and it was that summer, Queen Elizabeth at just twenty-seven had her coronation, signifying her divine right as sovereign and anointing her to the throne. The event was televised around the globe in nearly every country and watched by twenty-seven million people, a huge audience at the time.

It was ground-breaking to televise the coronation, the idea had been pushed by her husband, Prince Philip, whom she charged as the official chairman of the momentous historical event. Televising the coronation was vehemently opposed and resisted by the other members of the staid and conservative committee whose eyebrows and ire were already raised because they viewed the ceremony as sacred, not to mention, Prince Philip's involvement unwelcomed. In many respects it was a gamble placing her husband in charge and televising the event. Philip's hunch paid off because the coronation connected Queen Elizabeth to her subjects in exactly the way Prince Philip hoped that it would. In the end, she was grateful she placed her trust in him.

Elizabeth was just three years older than Jackie, but her advantage was that she had been preparing for her role as queen, since childhood. Jackie, as First Lady, had only a year to prepare, not knowing for certain that she would be saddled with her new position. When she married Jack, he was a senator not a president. She did not relish being First Lady, not at first. As First Lady she felt at times anxious, exhausted, and burdened but also exhilarated. The fit was becoming more comfortable as time passed.

For Elizabeth, it was inevitable that she would one day be queen. Philip understood the terms, yet still blamed his wife for his second-fiddle status. He compensated his station by using the position he did have by stretching it to its very limits.

Jackie and Elizabeth shared a deep affinity for dogs and horses. They were both horsewomen who rode with skill and regularity and they were both mothers of young children, but Jackie was more hands on while Elizabeth left child rearing to nannies and governesses.

How different the world had come to be in the 1960s. Jackie relished and celebrated the new modern decade. Jack and Jackie embodied the sixties. It was their time. Compared with Elizabeth, Jackie was free to indulge and was not bound by strict rules and guidelines. Jackie and JFK were

49

fortunate to be able to modernize and shape the White House to their own liking. The queen was still restricted and hampered by a strict royal protocol.

Cocktails on silver trays were served by footmen. The guests formed small groups each eyeing the Americans as JFK and Jackie made their way effortlessly around the room making conversation. By this time, JFK had been in office for nearly five months. As a couple, they had socializing and mingling down pat. It was nearly impossible not to be enchanted by them.

Prince Philip took two cocktails from a footman's tray. He handed one to Jackie. "May I call you, Jackie?"

"If I may call you, Philip," Jackie smiled sipping her drink. She was confident and flirty meaning to be playful.

Prince Philip was an attractive man who stood six feet tall, the same as her husband. Somehow, she thought he would be taller. Perhaps it was because Philip towered over his wife, who was just five foot four inches tall.

Ever charmed by an attractive woman, the prince answered, letting protocol fly out the window, "Certainly, it is what friends do, is it not?"

"Yes, it is" she said, relieved her instincts

paid off, however she never did take him up on his permission. "I hope that we'll be friends. Tell me, did it take long for you to get used to the palace?" Jackie asked, "I am stunned by the scale of it."

"Drafty as hell, this pile of bricks," Philip charmingly answered, smiling. "Before this we had a lovely house, more to human scale, but we had to go where the job took us," he smiled and shrugged.

"Do you ever get lost?" Jackie asked, then felt a bit silly.

"Not anymore but one corridor can look much like the next, I use paintings as markers," Philip sipped his cocktail.

"Of course, so long as the paintings aren't moved!" They both laughed. She continued, "I know what you mean about moving to where the job takes you. I have just begun the restoration for the Presidential Mansion. It is in a terrible state. To be honest, I don't think I could bear to live in the White House without bringing it back to its original glory."

"It will certainly be quite satisfying I imagine when you're finished. Before we moved to Buckingham, I was in the final stages of decorating a beautiful Georgian. It was a talent I discovered I didn't know I had." He smiled. "I was getting quite attached to the place, but life has a way of making

51

its own plans. Tell me, what's the best thing you enjoy about being First Lady?"

"Breakfast in bed," she laughed, then offered more pointedly, "Just as we got into office, I was able to save from the wrecking ball an historic building in Washington," Jackie offered, not without satisfaction.

"That's handy," the prince nodded. "Wouldn't it be more fun to just have people bring you things?" Philip asked with irony in his voice.

"To my amazement they do that, too." They both laughed. "Do people also bring you things?" Jackie smiled.

"If they don't, I can ask my wife to chop off their heads."

Gradually, others joined in, and they were able to mingle as they chose. Both Jackie and Jack tried their best to have a few words with most everyone. All seemed pleased to meet them and be in their company. So approachable, they made it easy. It was the American way and they embodied America, in the best sense.

When it was time, Prince Phillip was at Jackie's side offering an arm to bring her into dinner. Jack offered his arm to Elizabeth who, in turn, steered him to his place of honor, seated next to her on her right in the center of the table. Toasts were made.

Then Jack stood, and holding his glass, addressed the gathering, "Your Majesties, Queen Elizabeth and Prince Philip," he began "it is a great honor that you have bestowed upon me and Mrs. Kennedy in having this intimate dinner for us and your sixty closest friends."

Everyone laughed.

"We are touched by your friendship and kind hospitality and if you ever find yourselves in our neck of the woods, we hope that you'll drop by."

There was more laughter as the remark was taken with the juxtaposition, he intended. JFK had an instinct in knowing how to read an audience. He knew his comment would land especially as the mood in the candlelit room was jovial and everyone was in festive spirits and enjoying themselves.

Before drinking from his flute, Jack raised his glass and smiled directly at the queen, and he again raised his glass to Philip who was seated across the table from him.

"Before I take my seat, I hope that it isn't against protocol to express to you, Ma'am, just how lovely you look tonight."

It was difficult to charm the queen, she was not easily susceptible, but charmed she was. After clear consommé, Beef Wellington was served, followed by fresh strawberries and cream. The cocktails continued.

Jackie wondered about Princess Margaret's conspicuous absence, the only sibling of the Queen. She had been looking forward to meeting Margaret who possessed flair, in both personality and style. Jackie was certain she had asked Tish to communicate with the palace her specific request to have Margaret among the guests.

The evening finished; they returned to their hotel suite at The Savoy to retire.

Jack, while unzipping her gown, remarked, "You seemed to have fun tonight!"

Jackie tugged her full-length white gloves off and slipped her arms out of her dress. She stepped out of the dress and placed it on a bedroom chair and said, "More fun than I thought I'd have, but I still can't figure out why Princess Margaret missed the party."

Jack untied his tie and unbuttoned his shirt, "Apparently, divorce is a real bugaboo. You realize they made an exception for your divorced sister and Stash to be there evidently because this was a private party and not official."

"Hmmm, so it was either my sister or hers

that she would allow to attend. How queer. Maybe she thought Margaret would steal her thunder."

"Could be," Jack agreed.

"I didn't expect dancing! That was a nice surprise," Jackie remarked.

"You looked ravishing."

"Did I?" Jackie demurred, as she slipped on a cream-colored full-length silk nightgown with the thinnest of straps, confident that her gown had been the envy of every woman at the party.

The Hubert de Givenchy creation, a sleek silhouette in ice blue silk shantung was sleeveless and had a *décolleté bateau* neckline that skimmed her collar bone. The bodice fit like a glove, a tailored bow at the waist, the only detail. To give the dress her personal touch, she affixed two matching sparkling diamond brooches on each shoulder. The bell-shaped ballerina column skirt was hemmed to reveal shoes made from the same fabric. She wore long white opera gloves which she did not remove the entire evening. Her hairdresser, Alexandre, swept her hair on top of her head. Large statement-making drop, diamond earrings with accompanying diamond clips in her hair completed the jaw-dropping look.

For official engagements, the clothes she

wore, including the accessories, would be meticulously cataloged marking the date, the event name, and who was in attendance. It was imperative to Jackie that she have a record for both personal and historical use. A tag was also hung on the hanger of each item as it was stored with the date and the event clearly marked to make keeping track easier for her.

The queen, for her part, had chosen a new gown for the occasion but upon the arrival of the honored guests it became instantly apparent that she was no match for Mrs. Kennedy. Jackie catapulted into the new decade, the Queen sadly, left behind in one if not two decades. The queen's gown was her preferred formal evening silhouette and was a larkspur tulle crinoline in blue made by her court dressmaker, Norman Hartnell. The antebellum skirt, that required petticoats, harkened to the previous decade. The dress had a sleeveless pleated bodice and thick velvet straps. The effect was clumsy and did nothing to compliment her attractive slim figure. It was odd how a new dress could appear so dated. A photograph was taken to commemorate the occasion. Queen Elizabeth and Jackie stood in the middle with JFK on the queen's right and Prince Philip to Jackie's left. Both Kennedys appeared to be talking while the photo was snapped the moment captured for scrutiny until the end of time.

"How did you find Philip?" Jack stepped out of his trousers leaving them on the floor and sat on the bed removing his socks.

Jackie touched Jack's shoulders, he grabbed her by the waist and pulled her close. She answered, "Nervous at first but he warmed up. He's got a wicked sense of humor."

"Does he?" Jack steered her on the bed and lay beside her, kissing her neck. "Shall we leave the lights on, Mrs. Kennedy?"

"If you wish, Mr. President!" She said enveloping him in her arms.

The Mona Lisa

The European tour continued. At the Summit in Vienna, Jackie charmed the leader of the Soviet Union, Nikita Khrushchev. Jack not so much. Khrushchev wiped the floor with him. Jack found himself ill-prepared. The experience stung.

Before the summit, Charles de Gaulle, the President of France, had a dinner in the Kennedys' honor at Versailles, an event that was broadcast around the globe. From Agent Clint Hill's vantage point, he observed Jackie make quite an impression wherever she went. Hill was almost in awe that she was able to speak three foreign languages and that she spoke French with Mr. de Gaulle captivating him with her knowledge of French history. Mr. de Gaulle seemed to hang on her every word.

Khrushchev was also smitten with the First Lady and openly flirted. She enjoyed the attention and experienced a rush while conversing on an equal footing with these powerful men. She understood perfectly that she was the president's wife, but she felt appreciated as a person in her own right. She did not wait, like some wallflower, for conversation to be initiated. She was not intimidated, if anything she was exhilarated. At times, Jack would catch her out of the corner of his eye, exchange a glance with her, and send a wink her way.

She, like JFK, was driven to be the best she could be. The world was never more a stage than now, and not only was she on that stage, but she was up to the challenge. All her preparation for life seemed to lead her to this moment. She was more than ready. When Agent Hill learned that Jackie convinced the French to lend Leonardo da Vinci's masterpiece, the *Mona Lisa,* to America, he was not surprised. She wanted the American public to see it. It was Hill's understanding that plans were in the works to ship the painting and have it installed in the National Gallery in Washington.

It should be noted that the *Mona Lisa* had never left France, not since da Vinci took *her* there himself. Jackie's powers of persuasion were just another aspect of her personality. If Hill were honest, he at first thought being assigned to her detail was a demotion. He had to admit how very wrong he was. Because of the success of the tour, America strengthened her allies and cemented

European friendships. There was no question in the President's mind or anyone else's that Jackie had contributed more than anyone could have predicted. She took Europe by storm and America was all the better for it. Clint Hill came to realize quickly that the situation was not business as usual by any stretch. His job had changed and was ever-changing. Luckily, he was young enough and flexible enough to rise to the challenge. Perhaps his youth was one of the reasons he was chosen to be assigned to her. Close in age, it was possible that she would relate better to him than an older agent. Still getting to know him, she was becoming more comfortable in their relationship. However, comfortable she became she never broke protocol and always addressed him formally.

As she walked breezily to the car, Jackie put a scarf on her head and tied it at the back of her neck. She was in a buoyant mood.

"Good afternoon, Mr. Hill."

"Afternoon, Mrs. Kennedy. Ready for the drive?" Clint opened the front passenger door for her, and she slipped in. He shut the door.

"You have no idea how ready." She smiled.

Clint slid into the driver's seat and shut the door. Adjusting the rear-view-mirror, he started the car, double checked that there were no stray children in the vicinity and slowly pulled away from the house. As they moved down the drive, they passed other Compound family homes. Nieces and nephews playing on the grass waved. She waved back. One last check at the guard station gate and they left the grounds to join the public road.

"Just how far is Provincetown, Mr. Hill?"

"Fifty miles. Once we get on the main road, it won't take long."

Clint Hill had a wife and a son about Caroline's age, with that in mind, Jackie decided to relay something cute about her daughter. "While I was getting ready, Caroline sat with me at my vanity and powdered her nose, monkey-see, monkey-do!"

Clint smiled.

"Caroline came with us when we went with the President on Saturday to the town center. She wanted a gum- ball and asked her daddy for a penny."

Jackie was all ears. Clint took a pack of cigarettes from his shirt pocket and offered Jackie the pack. She took it, turned it on its side and gave a decisive tap. A cigarette popped out, she took it and tapped the pack again. He took back the pack and grabbed the cigarette with his mouth. He replaced the pack in his pocket.

"We'd better roll up the windows for a minute."

Jackie rolled up hers, turning the crank as Clint did his side. He reached in his shirt pocket for his lighter and lit her cigarette first, then his. Exhaling, they each rolled down their windows a third of the way.

"Did the President give Caroline a penny?" Jackie smirked.

"Not exactly. First, he had to tell Caroline that the gumball cost a penny and he didn't have one. Her face just about crumbled until Agent Landis reached into his pocket for some change. He let Caroline choose the coin."

Jackie nodded, "Did she choose correctly?"

"She did and thanked him even called him, Mr. Landis, just as you instructed."

"That makes me happy." Jackie smiled.

"She had a little trouble getting the penny in the slot. The President helped her turn the knob and when the gum rolled out, she popped it in her mouth as pleased as she could be."

"What did the President say?" Jackie asked.

"Mr. Landis, I owe you a penny." They both laughed.

"Where did the President come up with Caroline's nickname?"

"You mean, Buttons?" Jackie asked. Clint nodded. "From her button nose, of course," adding, "You must think it awfully ironic that the President never has any money with him?"

Clint laughed, "I can't say it hasn't crossed my mind."

On Sundays at church, when the collection basket came around, without fail JFK would turn around with a look of expectation on his face. Invariably, one of his details would hand him a twenty-dollar bill that he would drop in the collection basket and just as important, JFK always made a point to repay the agent later in the day.

Jackie crossed her right leg over her left and rested her shoulder against the back of the seat. She took great pleasure in smoking with nothing more on her mind than the immediate plans.

"Tell me, what was it like growing up in North Dakota?"

She drew on the cigarette and was careful to blow the smoke out the window. Clint was not exactly surprised by the question. He found the First Lady to be inquisitive and an excellent conversationalist. Naturally, there were many times when they were together and there was no conversation at all. Often preoccupied, she was lost in her own thoughts. This afternoon she was relaxed and with more than an hour's drive before them, talking was a good way to pass the time. Besides Jackie was curious and what better way to get to know someone than to ask pointed questions.

"I think more people attended your wedding than lived in my town." He glanced over at her to see her reaction. She only nodded waiting for more. "I have an older sister. Our house was small, so I didn't have my own room. My grandfather lived with us, and I shared the porch with him."

"Did you like your grandfather?"

"Oh, for sure. We had many nice conversations in the dark looking at the stars. I realize now if we hadn't shared that space, I probably wouldn't have got to know him so well."

"I imagine that is so. There is always a silver lining, Mr. Hill. Weren't you cold in the winter?" Jackie asked intrigued.

"I learned to dress pretty fast, I can tell you that," he smiled. "We had lots of blankets, so it wasn't so bad. I was used to it. Summers were hot and humid. I learned to swim and canoe in the Missouri River."

"Too bad you never learned to water ski," Jackie added wryly.

She had recently given Clint his first water skiing lessons. All of them ending abysmally from his point of view. It was especially mortifying, since Jackie water skied not only effortlessly, but when she wanted, did it on one ski.

Clint laughed. "Don't give up on me. I'm going to die trying!"

"I think you will." They both laughed. "You can be honest. After guarding President Eisenhower, you must have thought being assigned to me was a bit of a demotion?"

Clint sat up and straightened his posture. "Mind a little music?" He asked.

Jackie nodded yes toward the radio and Clint switched it on. *Mamma Said There'd be Days Like This* by the Shirelles played. He stubbed out his cigarette in the car ashtray. Jackie did the same.

"Honestly, I didn't know what to expect. I imagined something much different from how the job's turned out. I pictured ladies' luncheons and lots of fashion shows. Boy, was I wrong!"

Jackie was smiling in rapt attention. She leaned against the car door and rested a bent leg on the seat.

Clint continued, "After the election, when I was being interviewed for my next assignment, I couldn't understand why they asked me if I could ride a horse or if I could water ski? ...Now, I know!" They both laughed.

Jackie did not just ride horses; she was what was known as an equestrian. She had been on horses since the age of three and had won many competitions. When she was a child, Jackie appeared in society columns in full riding apparel either on horseback or standing next to her elegant father, Black Jack Bouvier who got the nickname from his deep tan and swarthy good looks. It had been in a fashionable New York City apartment on Park Avenue that she grew up and it was her good fortune to have a first-class education. As was the custom for girls of her social class, she completed her formal education in a prestigious finishing school in Connecticut.

Clint Hill was aware that the worlds they came from were vastly different. How odd it was that the lives of two people with upbringings as different as theirs having opposite backgrounds could converge without rhyme or reason? He was certain it was something he gave more thought to than she. Never in a million years could he have imagined that he would land here in this place at this time. It was worlds away from where he grew up in Washburn, North Dakota.

Continuing his explanation about being

reassigned to her detail he confessed, "I thought I had done something wrong."

They both laughed.

Jackie added, "I can see why," she smiled, "If it's any consolation, the job isn't what I imagined either and I don't even get paid."

They both laughed.

"I traveled with President Eisenhower who was popular and attracted crowds, but I've never seen crowds like the ones that congregated in Paris for you and the President," Clint remarked.

"My dresses were prettier," Jackie smirked with her tongue lodged in her cheek and her eyebrows raised. Clint laughed.

"Did you realize the estimate for the Paris crowds were two-hundred-fifty-thousand people?"

"Gosh! That *is* a lot of people. The President was thrilled. The French are such lovely and friendly people. I don't think I'll ever forget it." Jackie chewed her thumb nail and smiled.

"Friendly? They were adoring!" Mr. Hill confirmed.

Jackie's smile broadened and her eyes brightened, "I'm crazy for France. I love *everything* about it, the country, the people, the food. I especially *love* their history. Eighteenth century

France is particularly fascinating to me. When I studied in Paris my junior year at Vassar, I lived with a family, and that certainly immersed me in the culture. That's when I really became fluent in the language."

Upon first arriving and living with the other students in a spartan dormitory during her semester abroad, Jackie saw a note on a school bulletin board offering accommodations with a French family. She quickly grabbed the note from the board and hightailed it to the address. Soon after, she found herself living with the aristocratic Comtesse Guyot de Renty, who lived in the genteel 16th arrondissement on Avenue Mozart with her son and a daughter who was exactly Jackie's age.

"That must have been wonderful for you living with a family," Clint said.

"Oh, it was so amazing, a truly enriching experience. I lived with a widowed countess and her son and daughter near the Arc de Triomphe. It wasn't as luxurious as it sounds even though the apartment was very grand and so was the neighborhood. This was just after the war and the countess was short on money, so she took in students to help make ends meet. There was no heat and barely any wood for the fireplaces. I can certainly relate to your story of sleeping in the cold. Of course, I was roughing it, we were seven in the apartment with only one bathroom, but I hardly noticed I was so over the moon to be twenty and in Paris. It was everything I dreamed and more."

"Sounds like a fascinating experience."

"It was. I would ask the countess to come with me to museums knowing that she didn't speak a word of English, so it forced me to practice my French. I learned so much from her but the biggest lessons she taught me were graciousness and humility."

It was a heady time for the young Jackie, a time of transformation. For her, France became a compass.

"I believe there are lessons we must learn in this life Mr. Hill and it's important to be receptive don't you agree?" Jackie asked.

"I haven't thought about it, not in that way," Clint smiled.

"I'm glad you came to Italy with me. Did you manage to have any fun?" Jackie asked.

"Almost drowning in the Bay of Naples comes to mind. Thanks for turning the boat around to haul out my sorry carcass!" Clint laughed.

Jackie laughed too, "That was *good* of me!" and adding with a glint in her eye, "And when I ditched you in Athens?"

"By jumping in the prince's sports car for a hair-raising speed chase?" Clint finished the sentence for her.

'That was fun!" Jackie laughed.

"For you!" Clint said wide-eyed shaking his head. "Now, I know better!"

"Then what, Mr. Hill, to *trust* me?" Jackie laughed, "You should have seen your face, all determined. That old Greek Colonel had steam coming out of his ears!" Jackie was in hysterics.

Clint laughed too. "I'm beginning to get the picture about what I can learn from you, Mrs. Kennedy," Clint smiled, and Jackie laughed.

Jackie knew it was wrong but without giving it a second thought she was in the sports car and speeding away. It was a risk, a fun memory of a wild speed chase and the satisfaction she had of outsmarting her Security Detail. Who was going to chastise her? The prince paid the price. He was the one who had to ride back to the palace with a colonel berating him shaking with rage, the veins in his neck bulging. She meant no harm and she believed if Mr. Hill got into any trouble, she would fix it. Deep down, he realized this and saw the incident from her point of view.

Clint Hill, ever serious and duty bound, was beginning to assess life from a different vantage point. Not thrilled when it occurred, when all was said and done, he was grateful to keep his post and grateful that the prince, young as he was, had skill as a driver.

"Isn't life just fascinating, Mr. Hill? I think it's wonderful that we don't know what comes next." Jackie straightened in her seat, placed her feet back on the floor and faced front enjoying the drive.

"They've told you that I have been invited to India?" She smiled.

"Yes, I've been told." He took his eyes off the road for a moment to glance at her.

"Oh, I can hardly wait. I just know it's going to be fascinating, wondrous and mysterious," Jackie said dreamily.

"And I'm hoping nobody's heard of you," he said with a smirk.

Scrub Pines & Weathered Shingles

Most of the drive on Route 6, the main road, was monotonous. Modest vintage Victorian farmhouses or Cape Cod style houses dotted the road, but they were few and far between. Occasionally, a roadside motel would suddenly appear, or small vacation cabins lined up in a row could be seen near each other in wooded areas. Some cabins looked small; big enough to contain a bed, maybe a bedside table, but not much else. Sometimes, they saw a farm stand selling freshly picked corn, ripe red tomatoes, peaches, watermelon, and summer squash. They noticed a hand painted "Antiques" sign which really meant, old but not particularly valuable furniture, old dishes, mostly bad paintings, old toys, and curiosities. Just the sort of musty shop that was fun to comb through on a rainy day.

Lining the highway were tall scrub pines and oaks. Trees that were indigenous to Cape Cod and survived well in dry sandy soil and New England's harsh winters. The scrub pines could be especially beautiful if you saw one on its own, isolated from the rest. The wind sometimes turned the tree's trunk as it grew to form a graceful shape like a tree in a Japanese watercolor. Also, growing wild along the road, were Concord grape vines and roses. Every now and then, they would pass an ancient graveyard with thin dark shale gravestones. The smallest of them would be white limestone and marked not with a name but with, "baby," "son," or "daughter."

"Are we nearly there? Time flies when you're having fun," Jackie remarked. "You know the Pilgrims landed first in Provincetown before they moved on to Plymouth?"

"I don't think I knew that."

"I've never been before but I've heard it's a very colorful place. Many famous people have spent time there, the dancer, Isadora Duncan, and the actor, Marlon Brando." She ticked off a list tapping her fingers as she continued, "Painters; Jackson Pollock, Robert Motherwell, Willem de Kooning, Hans Hofmann, and writers; Eugene O'Neill, Tennessee Williams, and Norman Mailer. Surely, some of these names ring a bell, Mr. Hill?" She smiled.

"Some ring a bell," he answered realizing he had some catching up to do regarding the 20th century art world.

"With such an illustrious history, it's high time I saw Provincetown for myself," Jackie mused. The radio played *Runaway* by Del Shannon. "Oh, this is a fun song isn't it, Mr. Hill?"

As they approached Provincetown, the road veered slightly and instead of continuing up an incline, the car began its descent. They were going down a steep hill which would soon flatten out.

"Oh, look, how beautiful the view is with the water on both sides," she observed.

Clint agreed. "According to the map when we come to Provincetown, Commercial Street will take us through the town. The motel should be at the end."

"I'm in your capable hands, Mr. Hill."

Surveying both sides of the street as they entered Commercial Street, Provincetown's main road, Jackie remarked, "Charming beach houses. They look so quintessentially New England, don't they, Mr. Hill? Wouldn't you just love to have one?"

Most were painted white or had naturally weathered cedar shingles with painted shutters. Some shutters were gray, some blue. Red was popular, so was dark green, and occasionally turquoise. The houses varied in size and vintage. They were built at varying periods in a staggering time frame, dating from the 1700s to the 1940s.

"Which would you choose?" Jackie inquired.

"One with a porch would be very nice," Clint smiled.

"I agree. You could have your coffee and read the newspaper and not have a care in the world. Oh look, what do you think of those shutters with the whale motif? I think they really work, don't you?"

Clint nodded and added, "When I buy that house, I won't change anything."

"I think that's a very good plan," Jackie smiled.

They rode along in silence for a bit, taking in the sights. The houses with accompanying gardens began to unfold. People on bicycles weaved past and there were people walking dogs, pushing baby carriages, or just enjoying a stroll.

Looking to the right and pointing, Jackie said, "Look at that church. Oh, it isn't a church, but it used to be, the sign says Chrysler Museum. I heard Walter Chrysler was opening a museum down here." She lowered the window all the way to get a better look. Speaking mainly to herself she said aloud, "I wonder if Mr. Vidal has had a chance to see Walter's art collection?"

They passed shops, some nicer than others. Some were honkytonk, selling tee shirts, shot glasses, coffee mugs, and key chains. These were popular with tourists as keepsakes did not cost much. There were straw hats and beach apparel shops, an art supplies store too, and suddenly a hardware store.

Jackie commented, "A hardware store makes you realize people really live here. Oh look, Mr. Hill, art galleries. So Bohemian! You know this is an artists' colony!"

"I knew it had that reputation," Clint agreed.

Turning around to get a better look she asked, "Are those two men holding hands?"

"In some cultures, men hold hands to express friendship." Clint added not without a bit or irony.

"Yes, Mr. Hill I am sure you are correct," playing along but not fooled, Jackie smiled, "but I don't think that's the case here."

They saw fresh fish being delivered. She turned around to look. Then facing front added, "Those were some big lobsters."

She spied a storefront with colorfully painted furniture that resembled Pennsylvania Dutch designs but were executed with more flair and sophistication, the sign read simply, 'Peter Hunt, Furniture.'

"Oh, how pretty. So darling. Perhaps it can be arranged for Mr. Hunt to come to Hyannis Port and show me some of his furniture. Will you make a note for me, Mr. Hill?"

"Yes. I'll remember," nodding Clint answered.

Commercial Street dipped a bit and at a Coast Guard station, Clint took a left-hand turn and followed the road bordered by the water which could be seen every so often between houses and small dwellings. There were small groups of people gathered on porches or sitting in chairs on lawns. The lucky residents had an empty lot across from them with nothing obstructing their water view. They breezed past more residential properties and the car climbed a slight hill then leveled. Jackie noticed a nicely situated hotel on the waterside with a pleasant garden that featured yellow day lilies that contrasted nicely against the backdrop of the hotel painted red and aptly named, The Red Inn.

"What a charming spot. I read President Teddy Roosevelt stayed at that very hotel." Jackie said. "The cocktail hour approaches. I can see why all the Adirondack chairs are taken. Just look at how the water sparkles."

"There's the marsh up ahead," Clint announced, "the motel should be across from it."

Turning right, Clint spotted The Moors Motel.

"We have arrived."

Clint drove into the property and finding a space, turned off the car.

"Ready when you are, Ma'am."

Jackie took a compact from her bag and set it on the dash. She rummaged a moment and found her lipstick. Opening both the tube and the compact she applied more frosted pink lipstick. She closed the tube, checked her teeth, and dropped both in her bag.

"All set. Let's go."

A View with a Room

Gore's motel room was located at the West End part of Provincetown outside the town center, in a place called, The Moors Motel. The Moors was a bit out of the way, quiet and a bit rustic. It had just a check-in reception desk and no lobby. Each room had a large picture window that showcased a beautiful view of marshy ocean and sea grass. Contrasted with an expansive deep blue sky and a splendid rock jetty, it proved a great spot and looked just as impressive, if not more so when the tide was out. During the day, there seemed to be an endless stream of adventurous beach goers who paraded through the marsh to get to the beach on the other side. When the tide was high, groups of mainly young men slogged through waist-high deep water balancing beach bags on their heads or shoulders. Making this journey, was part of the fun and adventure that a beach town like Provincetown offered. It was possible to drive a car to the beach, but what was the fun in that?

The marsh was alluring enough to attract painters who set up easels to while away the hours as they attempted to capture the ever-changing, dazzling Cape light as it reflected off the water and onto the landscape.

The motel room walls were painted white. Above the bed was a seascape painting of average quality. Much appreciated were two bedside lamps on tables that flanked the bed. Both Gore and Howard had a stack of books on their side of the bed and at night enjoyed reading before turning out the lights. Some books they brought with them others they bought at the local book shops. A floor lamp stood next to a wingback chair. The chair stood near the picture window. A table served as a desk. There was also a chest with four drawers. The table had a full-size ceramic lamp with a linen shade. A typewriter sat on the table with more books and yellow legal pads. Gore used a mug as a pencil holder.

Even on vacation, Gore was working, always writing. Even when he was not writing he was thinking about what he was working on. Ideas were always swirling in his mind to be recalled as he determined how to precisely present his thoughts.

The hardwood floor had a braided rag rug. It was nearly impossible to keep the floor sand-free even after it had been cleaned for the day. Various clothing items hung casually from wall hooks, khaki trousers, denim jeans, a pair of shorts, a shirt, and a jacket. On a shelf, above the hooks, were a pair of white canvas sneakers and a straw hat, both of which, were well worn. Conveniently, there was a closet big enough to stow suitcases that Gore and Howard took full advantage of. They were staying in Provincetown for over a month and liked to have an orderly environment. There was little reason to have two rooms. For the most part, Howard was out and about walking the town and meeting friends and that allowed Gore to have the quiet to work as he needed.

Gore was looking forward to showing Jackie Provincetown. Their friendship had been evolving for some time. Back when Jack was a senator, Gore had enjoyed dinners at their home in Georgetown. Intimate dinners, with interesting people, where the conversation and the booze flowed. Welcomed on his own terms, Gore did not have to sing for his supper like fellow writer, Truman Capote who acted like a mascot for wealthy society ladies in Manhattan. His dislike for Capote was both personal and professional. Capote, he felt, was an upstart, a notorious social climber, and in the habit of using people and situations for his own advantage. Gore was not wrong in his assessment.

Capote had come from humble roots, and not being well-bred had to claw his way to the top of the heap. Truman thought of himself as an exotic creature, convincing himself that he was in high demand. In the circles Truman traveled he was not wrong; he was in demand. He made friends with the wives of powerful men; women who looked forward to long gossipy lunches. To them, Truman was exotic and amusing. Comparatively speaking, as matrons, even as beautiful and sophisticated as they were, their staid lives adhered to strict rules of etiquette, decorum, and social strata. Truman added spark. These women of privilege were bred to make good marriages and while the world was open to them, the code they clung to was restrictive. Truman added color because he observed and commented on his observations. He said things they may have wanted to say but would not or simply could not.

At the same time, Truman knew while the wives adored him, the husbands simply tolerated him. He may have been foolish at times, but stupid he was not. Still in possession of a driving ambition, Truman, for a time, was able to separate his two worlds, making a distinction between work and play, careful not to mix them.

Gore never stooped to what he considered

Capote's demeaning level. He did not consider his sexuality a talking point or even a particular characteristic of who he was. He did not allow this aspect of his sexuality to define him. Nor was he ashamed. On the contrary. He was just a man who preferred sex with other men, and he felt it was the most natural thing in the world. Vidal was the antithesis of Capote. He was tall, handsome and in his youth, considered something of an Adonis.

At present, he felt he was entering his prime. Dressed simply in fitted khaki trousers, a blue stripe shirt, a rope belt and driving loafers without socks, he looked attractive and felt comfortable. Gore had been a man who was not interested in clothes or having a wardrobe to speak of, until recently. Clothes, he had thought were serviceable. After the war, when he was back to being a civilian, he had just one suit that he wore until the backside and elbows were worn to a sheen. Eventually, his publisher had to encourage him to breakdown and buy another suit.

The beach suited him. He loved being comfortable and casual but realized he could be both and still wear attractive clothes which fit. It was a revelation realizing it took almost the same amount of effort to put on ratty clothes as it did smart clothes. Besides, he wanted to look nice for Jackie.

She had that effect on people. Consequently, he tried looking a bit more jaunty than usual donning the rope-belt his companion, Howard, bought him earlier in the week in one of the local shops.

Absorbed in his book, still he was not unaware that the time approached. Moments later there was a firm knock on the door. Gore got up from the chair, walked to the door and turned the doorknob. Opening the door wide, he greeted them.

"Well, hello I see you found me."

Embracing Gore warmly and entering the room Jackie offered, "Mr. Hill could suss out a speakeasy in Berlin."

She removed her scarf and ran a hand through her hair.

Gore shook Clint's hand, "Hello Mr. Hill, nice to see you. Would you like to come in?" He offered warmly.

"No thanks," Clint responded to the invitation. Speaking to Jackie he said, "I'll wait for you out here."

Gore smiled and nodded, "Mr. Hill please excuse us."

Closing the door and turning to face Jackie, Gore gestured toward the large picture window, "Welcome to my room and to Provincetown." He exclaimed, "Isn't the view spectacular?"

"Very." Jackie shook her head affirmatively, yes. "By the way, nice loafers." Nothing escaped Jackie's keen eye.

Gore looked down at his shoes, "Gee, thanks. I thought they were nice." Continuing 'the tour' Gore said, "The room is basic, as you can plainly see. But the marsh," he gestured "that's the thing. The view changes constantly with the tides and the light."

The light at this time of day in summer was almost indescribable bouncing a warm glow and bathing everything it shone in a surreal hyper-bright light that reflected off the water. He allowed for Jackie to fully appreciate the scene before her as if a painting framed by the window.

"You know an interesting fact" Gore continued, "the Pilgrims landed just across from here beyond the marsh." Extending an arm, he pointed, "Right about there."

"Isn't that fascinating," Jackie remarked, "that their specific point of entry is known and documented? I wonder what they'd make of the village now?" she smiled.

"Undoubtedly, the Pilgrims would be amazed."

"It's the Puritans who would be horrified!"

85

Jackie added. They both laughed.

    Jackie sat on the bed and happily bounced up and down. "What a view to wake up to." She said and looking at Gore added, "I'm so happy to be here. We drove the main street from start to finish. Provincetown is simply charming. I can't believe I've never been here."

    "See, I didn't exaggerate, I knew you would like it!"

    "I do like it. I saw men holding hands!"

    "Yes," Gore nodded, "There's a lot of that. The locals are tolerant. They got used to a variety of people through the decades. Provincetown has been an art colony since 1890." Gore turned the desk chair around and sat. "I was supposed to work this morning but instead Howard and I rode bikes to Race Point beach. We spent the morning there and we swam nude." He smiled then he remembered to ask, "Are you thirsty, I can offer you a glass of H2O."

    "No thanks, I'm fine. Swimming nude sounds quite liberating. Gosh, you must be careful not to burn." She smiled back.

    "I tan easily. Howard must be more cautious."

    "Is Howard enjoying Provincetown too?"

    "Yes, loves it. He's with some friends today."

    "Gore, just how long have you and Howard

been together?"

"Well, let me think. I believe it's ten years. Quite a while."

"I was wondering. I hope you don't mind me asking you a question?"

"Ask whatever your heart's desire. Bombs away!"

"Well, it's just that...I hope, I know this is personal, I was wondering are you and Howard monogamous?" Jackie asked a little timidly.

"Oh, are you curious?" Gore was taken aback but only slightly.

"Well, yes," she said, "I admit to having a certain curiosity but it's more than that. I wonder if men are capable of honest-to- goodness fidelity?" Jackie offered more of an explanation by adding, "God knows my father wasn't! If you can believe it, Daddy told me that on my parents' honeymoon, he went to bed with Doris Duke."

"The tobacco heiress?" Gore guessed.

Jackie nodded.After the disclosure, Jackie laughed, half out of embarrassment and half from sheer incredulousness.

"Well, now! We have more in common than I imagined. Only it was my mother who was the philanderer, not my father." Gore remarked. "An utter hedonist who knew no particular boundaries or didn't think they applied to her. She once brought her Negro taxi driver into the house for an afternoon of sexual escapades."

"That was risky," Jackie said wide-eyed.

"Reckless is more like it and on so many levels!" Gore clarified.

"I think it's a well-known fact that my father was a notorious ladies' man," Jackie said, adding, "at that time, it was almost unheard of when my parents divorced and on a certain level it made me ashamed. The marriage was already on shaky ground, and I think what put the final nail in the coffin, was when a society page published a photograph of my parents and another woman. Daddy was standing between them holding hands. The trouble came because the hand he held was not my mother's."

"Oops!" Gore interjected.

Jackie nodded knowingly and continued, "Daddy and this woman mistakenly thought that their holding hands would go undetected by my mother specifically and the world generally. That picture was seen by everyone, and it was the last straw."

"Not shocking that the divorce came after such a public humiliation. I have found that behind closed doors people are willing to put up with almost anything but once, whatever it is, is no longer private, it becomes a different matter entirely," Gore reasoned.

"You can say that again, all hell broke loose," Jackie admitted. "The oddest thing came later." Jackie feeling comfortable divulged, "It was Daddy's habit to point out to me in the club restaurant or ballroom women with whom he'd had his 'way.'"

"And here I thought, it would be me imparting juicy details," Gore laughed.

"I know I should have been scandalized, but if I'm honest I was intrigued," Jackie confessed.

"It amazes me how unaware our parent's generation could be of trampling boundaries willy-nilly," Gore interjected.

"All I can think is maybe he thought imparting these secrets would bring us closer," Jackie reasoned.

"It's as if this notion of appropriateness escaped them. Our grandparents looked at this sort of thing so differently. Maybe they were wiser. I just don't know," Gore pondered.

"My father, being so dapper, impressed my school chums. He was charming and charismatic and was always impeccably dressed. He'd take me and them to lunch in the city to fancy restaurants. I'd get a kick out of watching them flirt with him."

"Black Jack did have what was known as "it!" He was a very attractive man. But let's not forget your question about fidelity and all. I realize I'm still on the hook."

"Yes, you are!"

Gore took a moment to ponder exactly how to phrase the rest of his response. "I'm not exactly the right man to answer your question. I have some theories on whether men are capable of fidelity. I am sure there are some," he said pausing. "I am surmising, your question is, have I had sex with other men and, does Howard know about it?"

"Yes, I suppose that's what I want to know." Her eyes were riveted on him. She wet her lips and pressed them together in anticipation of his answer.

Gore answered methodically, "Howard and I don't sleep together!" He paused to let that fact sink in. "Really... we never did. Sexually speaking, he's not my type. We have an understanding. We do as we please, and we don't ask questions of each other." Jackie was fascinated. Smiling, he finished with, "I'm not Howard's type, either."

"But" said Jackie, tilting her head and trying to understand, "you consider yourselves...think of yourselves as a couple? Certainly, I think of you that way."

"Thanks." Gore smiled, "You are a most extraordinary and modern woman." Gore placed his folded arms on top of the chair back. "Yes, we are a couple. Very much so."

"If your relationship is not sexual, what keeps you together, do you think?"

"We're friends. Maybe... life companions." Gore leaned back against the table and placed his hands behind his head making himself more comfortable.

Jackie leaned back on the bed, supporting herself with her elbows. She put a foot on the bedspread.

Gore continued, "From the moment I met Howard, I felt comfortable and easy with him. He is everything I was brought up to be prejudiced against. He's Jewish and when we met, he was uneducated and working-class Brooklyn. Still, we were drawn to each other. There was an unspoken kinship that we could be the family neither of us had."

Jackie was wide-eyed, captivated as she listened. Very few people she knew laid their cards out on the table like this. She nodded, as if to say, how interesting!

"When Howard was 17, his parents found

out he was homosexual and threw him out of the house. It was devastating for him. He does not come from landed gentry like some of us. He comes from Queens, for Chrissake!"

"How horrible!" Jackie responded.

"How horrible that he was cast out or that he's from Queens?" Gore smiled devilishly.

"Oh, you!" Jackie sat up and got off the bed. She walked over to his desk and fingered the books. She turned to face him, "Thank you for being honest."

Gore smiled. "Oh, it's fine. I don't often discuss my private life but we're family...of sorts." Changing gears, he asked, "Did Jack like the books I sent?"

"He's enjoying your book, *Messiah* very much. The collapse and destruction of Christianity is a far cry from his usual political reading."

"I imagine it is," Gore laughed.

She cocked her head, "Usually Jack enjoys espionage novels and history books." She leaned against the table and rested her hands on the surface and continued, "Jack's a history buff, like you, and an expert on his boyhood hero, Winston Churchill."

Gore crossed his legs. "I can see that!"

"Did you know not long after we were married, we met Churchill on Aristotle Onassis's yacht?" Jackie paused, then smiled, "We were vacationing on the Côte d'Azur. Winston was Aristotle's guest of honor."

"That must have been thrilling for Jack."

"Well, it should have been, but Churchill spent most of his time talking to me and Ari." Jackie paused for impact. "Jack was wearing a white dinner jacket. I told Jack, maybe Churchill thought he was one of the waiters. Jack was not amused."

Gore laughed. "I can see why Jack was not amused. What about you? What have you been reading?"

Matter-of-factly, Jackie answered, "Proust, Kerouac. I'm in the middle of *Casanova's Memoirs*. Can you imagine, twelve volumes? That man got around." Rather animatedly, she added, "Casanova died in what was the Austrian Empire, now Czechoslovakia! That surprised me. His memoirs give a vivid description of 18th century court life." Jackie clasped her hands to her chest said, "You know this period in history has such personal fascination for me. I devoured *Memoirs du Duc de Saint-Simon.*"

Gore asked, "In French?"

Rather blasé, "Yes, of course."

Running her hands through her hair and glancing in a mirror, Jackie blurted, "I've rethought the wig idea. Maybe I don't need a disguise. It might draw more attention, don't you think?" She asked squinting. "Maybe just a scarf and these sunglasses."

She pulled her sunglasses from her bag and fiddled with them. "After all, we did drive the length of the town without one person even looking at me... It was heaven."

She flopped back down on the bed.

Gore smiled, "Yes, I imagine it must have been wonderful not to be recognized."

Getting up from his chair, "By the way, I decided we'll have dinner at The Flagship. It's the place to go. They have a nice menu, and the harbor views are very pleasing."

"And the play, are we within walking distance to the playhouse?"

"Yes, we will be after dinner, it's very near the restaurant, if you feel like walking now?" Gore asked. "I got us tickets for the George Bernard Shaw play, *Mrs. Warren's Profession.*"

Jackie smirked asking, "Her profession? Remind me, is what exactly?"

"She's a prostitute!"

They both burst into laughter.

"Perfect. My mother-in-law accuses me of only liking whatever is on the Catholic Church's forbidden list. This is rich!"

"Off to a blazing start. Shall we?" Gore suggested.

Jackie got up from the bed, put her scarf back on, but this time tied it under her chin adjusting it to expose more of her hair. She grabbed her purse and took one last look in the mirror. They exited the room and joined Mr. Hill in the hallway.

Especially taking pains to make Clint aware Gore explained, "The restaurant is a good thirty-minute walk from here. It is almost at the other end of town. Still want to hoof it?" he asked Jackie.

"I'm sick to death of being driven everywhere. Let's walk!"

Jackie made eye contact with Mr. Hill. She tilted her head with a light jerk as if to say, "Let's go!"

SALEMS NOT GAULOISES

Gore offered a chivalrous arm. They walked out of The Moors Motel grounds making their way down the driveway. Bearing left onto Commercial Street, they backtracked on foot the same way Jackie and Clint had driven. The tide was out and in this part of the bay, the ocean bed drained exposing large rocks and left sporadic thin rivulets of water. This happened at different intervals. Luckily, the fish swam out with the tide, because there was no evidence of dead fish left in the bed. Certainly, no fish that Gore had noticed when he walked the jetty at different times of the day.

There was no sidewalk for a stretch. By the road, they encountered sandy soil that supported Dusty Miller, a plant that thrived in sandy soil, beach grass, and beach roses. Gore explained that walking this way was safer and more picturesque than the busier Bradford. Soon there would be a sidewalk and upon reaching it, Jackie held onto Gore's shoulder balancing herself while she removed each sandal and brushed her feet of sand. They continued from the West End almost the entire length of Provincetown, but not quite the full two miles. At the beginning and further from the center of town, they did not encounter many people.

Clint Hill was adept as maintaining a respectful distance yet close enough to spring into action if the situation warranted especially as they encountered more people. He was watchful, hyper-aware of a change in dynamics as he looked for evidence on faces, a flash of recognition in their eyes.

Jackie was relaxed and happy, so far, the town seemed unaware of who was in their midst as she walked the street as if she were ordinary. At present, she was. Linking Gore's arm with hers, they conversed about the gardens, the architecture, and resisting the temptation, avoided people walking their dogs. As they got closer to the town center, the throngs grew thicker with high-spirited people of all ages, but the trio of Gore, Jackie and Clint following closely behind were hardly mingling among them.

The vacation season was coming to an end. The Labor Day holiday would be early this year signaling a death rattle to summer fun. As they ambled along with purpose, they passed other people and pretended to be deep in conversation or Gore would extend his arm, blocking Jackie's face to point to an architectural detail. It was fun hiding in plain sight.

"What are these small one room cabins we keep seeing?" Jackie asked.

"Fishermen's houses," Gore informed. "I'm not exactly sure if they stay in them or just work in them."

Jackie did not say anything, but her eyes widened. Now that she knew what they were, she noticed more of them. If there was a window or a door open, she discreetly peered in. They rounded the bend bearing to the right. The water continued to be in view between the buildings and down alleyways.

The bigger houses, if you were lucky to get as a rental, had verandas so friends could engage in Provincetown's seasonal past time of cocktail drinking and people watching. Sometimes the groups were mixed, with both men and women, but mostly they were not. There were guest houses but more commonly vacationers rented a room from a resident who benefited by making a little income. Those on holiday were easy to spot because their attitude and demeanor were different from the townspeople who quietly went about their daily lives. The locals stayed close to home and kept to themselves especially in summer when the population swelled. Some owned local restaurants that featured Portuguese fare, and bakeries that made Portuguese bread, pastries, and fried dough.

Gore and Jackie passed these establishments on their way through town. There was an old-fashioned looking saltwater taffy store with large plate glass windows that had been in business since the 1900s. The charming architecture of the taffy shop instilled confidence that their taffy would surely be the best for miles around.

The shops, still aglow, were doing a brisk tee shirt and trinket business. There were more candy stores, an ice cream shop, a drug store with a soda fountain, several bookstores, a liquor store, and a newsstand. The biggest development approved and very welcomed by the town, was the recent A&P supermarket. A souvenir shop sold presidential items of the current First Family. Jackie saw herself and Jack's image on commemorative plates but what really tickled her were the ceramic JFKs sitting in rocking chairs. He was the salt; the chair was the pepper. Jackie laughed looking in the window when Gore pointed out the items to her.

"I'm going to send those to you," he said.

"Please don't," Jackie pretended to beg, jabbing him, playfully in the arm. Relenting she added laughing, proving she was a good sport, "well, if you must."

In the week that followed, a package from Gore arrived at The Compound. Contained in the box were two commemorative plates with their images, their heads floating in a white space in the middle of the plate, a presidential mug, and the salt and pepper shaker set. Upon seeing the ceramic JFK salter, little Caroline remarked shaking her head, "that doesn't look like my daddy."

Within no time, they arrived at the nautically themed, Flagship restaurant. Fishing nets and oars decorated the restaurant. Brass lanterns hung from the ceiling and lit kerosene hurricane lamps on each table created a warm atmosphere.

The three entered together. Clint separated from them and positioned himself on a corner stool at the bar. Jackie suggested he order himself a meal as they planned to be at their table a while. He appreciated the suggestion which was really permission. Most often he did not eat on the job. None of the agents did. They grabbed on the go. Sitting down to any meal was a luxury.

Gore asked the man in charge, "Mind if we seat ourselves over there?" pointing to a specific table.

Gore pulled out a chair and Jackie sat with her back facing the dining room. Clint easily kept an eye on the door and them. Once they were seated, Clint nodded in their direction. Gore caught his eye and nodded back and just for fun, imagined himself part of an undercover operation. He did not share this fantasy with his dining companion. Several customers were seated at the bar. Clint ordered fish and chips and a Coke.

"Hungry?" Gore asked.

"Starving suddenly. I could eat a horse." Rather thoughtfully she added, "What a terrible expression that is!" Jackie removed her scarf and placed her sunglasses on her head. She tied her scarf on the handle of her handbag.

Gore perused the menu, looked up and said, "Speaking of which, you took quite the header! Front page of the *Times* of you flying headfirst off your horse!"

"Oh, that! It was infuriating that they published that photo." Jackie shook her head.

"You have to admit; it was a spectacular shot!"

"I suppose it was. You know what Jack said?"

Gore intrigued, "Tell me." He raised an eyebrow.

Placing the menu against her chest; she said, feigning indignation, "He said, 'When the First Lady falls on her ass, it's news!'" She shook her head. "That man!" They both laughed.

"The photographer," who had been hiding in the bushes, "sent Jack a framed blow-up," Jackie admitted.

"How marvelous! Did he include a note so you could send a thank you?"

Jackie smiled and shook her head. "Do you think I could have a gin and tonic?"

"I don't see why not. It's past five o'clock! As if that matters," he laughed. "I'll order for us if you like, do mussels sound appealing?"

Jackie nodded yes in agreement.

Gore summoned the waiter, a tall, slim, young man with parted sandy colored hair that almost covered one eye.

"Two gin and tonics, please. We'll each have clam chowder to begin and then linguini with mussels."

Closing his menu, he gave it to the waiter. The waiter collected Jackie's menu.

Before the waiter departed, Gore instructed, "Waiter, could you please bring the drinks first and some raw oysters? Please bring the oysters before the chowder. Oh, and Waiter, see that man sitting at the bar with the open collar green shirt? Whatever he orders add to my bill."

"Very good, Sir. I'll get the drinks for you, right away. A large order of oysters?"

"Yes, I think so," Gore inquired, "Wellfleet or Yarmouth?"

"Wellfleet," answered the waiter.

"Lucky us." Jackie remarked and removed her sunglasses from her head and fiddled with them. "I'm dying for a cigarette."

Gore remarked, "You know in Britain they call cigarettes 'fags.' Shall I choose one for you?" He smiled wickedly eyeing the other diners.

"Oh, you! Jack doesn't like me to smoke in public. He thinks it looks cheap. Undignified." Jackie chewed her thumb nail. "When I don't smoke, I chew my fingernails." Holding her hands out for inspection, "Look at my hands! They make me ashamed...I wear gloves."

"Well, you can't wear gloves with Capri pants, now, can you?" Surveying the room, "I don't think anyone's noticed you. Have a quick one if you want."

"Think so?" Rummaging in her bag, she pulled out a cigarette. Gore took a lighter from his pocket and lit it for her.

"Salems not Gauloises?" he teased.

Jackie smirked as she blew smoke toward the

ceiling. She rested her elbow on the table, better to keep the cigarette elevated. She smoked elegantly. There was nothing cheap or undignified about her. In that respect, Gore disagreed with Jack's assessment. Another woman might look cheap, but he was convinced, Jackie could make chewing gum look sophisticated.

The waiter brought the drinks. They clinked glasses and each took a sip.

"How are the children?"

Exhaling upward, Jackie answered, "Caroline told a reporter, 'Daddy's upstairs wearing no socks and no shoes and not doing anything at all.'"

Gore laughed. "Well, isn't she the little blabbermouth!"

"Tell me about it! Jack thought it was hilarious. Good thing too, because they printed it."

Gore quipped, "A writer must always tell the truth, unless he's a journalist."

"Ha-ha, very good," said Jackie, "Did you see this morning's paper? There's a picture of Jack with the very first Peace Corps volunteers."

"Really! So, the program *is* underway," Gore smiled, pleased. "You know there is no human problem that could not be solved if people would simply do as I advise."

Jackie laughed, "I realize you are kidding."

"Am I?" Gore jested; eyebrows raised.

Jackie exhaled leisurely, "Working on anything new?"

Gore nodded yes, "I'm beavering away on a book about the fourth century Roman Emperor, Julian."

"Ancient Rome? Hmmm, a comedy!" Jackie mused. "Writers, I'm told, write what they know. Do you ascribe to the notion of reincarnation?"

"Not exactly," Gore laughed, "Nothing gets past you." He pointed a finger at her.

"Ancient history and ancient Rome are something I have been interested in since childhood. Of course, it is historical fiction which makes it more palatable for the reader and of course, is more fun for me to write. I'll make it current and relevant to today's world. History does repeat itself," and he then added thoughtfully, "but is man capable of learning from it? What did Napoleon say, 'History is a set of lies agreed upon.'"

Jackie nodded, "Awful that horrible wall between East and West Berlin. One side freedom and the other side under an iron thumb."

"It's troubling." Gore said shaking his head. "After the war, the Allies punished Germany by dividing it in two. Now East Berlin is building the wall adding insult to injury! East Berlin will be a virtual prison, people locked in with no hope of escape. Trying to, will prove fatal."

"I shudder to think of it." Jackie added, "I've seen those guards on television, and they are armed to the teeth!" She shook her head.

"The world's problems must keep Jack up at night. A heavy burden to say the least." Gore said, sipping his cocktail.

"Jack feels the weight of it. We've talked about it. Should an atom bomb be dropped, Washington will surely be a target."

"It is a sobering topic. Let's hope the Cold War doesn't get hot!" Sipping his drink and then setting it on the table, Gore fiddled with a paper straw.

The waiter approached their table, "Oysters from Wellfleet, Mrs. Ken...?"

Looking up at the waiter, Jackie shook her head ever so slightly and placed a finger to her mouth.

The waiter instantly understood discretion was called for, "I'll bring the chowder in a bit."

"Thank you," Gore said dismissing the waiter for the moment but not curtly. Turning back to Jackie asked, "Making progress on the house with the columns?"

While he anticipated her answer, he chose a large juicy oyster from his side of the platter, which was layered with ice, sliced lemon wedges, and a small bowl of mignonette sauce in the center. He squeezed a bit of lemon on the oyster and with the small serving spoon added a bit of the sauce. He brought the shell to his mouth, tilted his head back to let the oyster slide in. It tasted briny, like the ocean. He chewed it before letting it slide down his throat.

In answer to Gore's question regarding the restoration of the White House, Jackie laughed, "I got rid of what I call Mamie Eisenhower pink. Gosh, it was just dreadful and there was so much of it. How are the oysters?" Jackie asked preparing her first.

"Divine," came the answer.

Continuing, she said, "Would you believe the Eisenhowers had La-Z-Boy recliners, and two televisions mounted into the wall so they could each watch their own programs? The televisions looked like two portholes!" They both laughed.

Picking up his glass in a toast gesture, Gore said, "To Ike and Mamie!"

Laughing, Jackie and Gore clinked glasses.

The House with the Columns

Jackie sipped her cocktail. The gin was nice quality having a tang of strong juniper berry. Wasn't it odd, she thought, that a liquor could be made from something that was not, strictly speaking, edible?

She was eager to impart some White House lore, "You'd be astounded to realize how swiftly an army of White House staff moves one family out and another one in. All of it happens during the inauguration."

"I wondered how it all came about," Gore gave her a side glance and moved in closer.

"It was a while before the family quarters were done but the children's rooms were ready that day and thank God *that* pink was gone. Jack slept in the Lincoln bedroom until our quarters were finally worked out."

"And what about you, where did you sleep?" Gore asked, curious.

"The Queen's bedroom," Jackie smiled a bit sheepishly realizing how that sounded.

Gore laughed, "Oh, now, the queen's room,

that's fitting!"

Jackie laughed. "Well, why not? It happens to be quite a nice room and it's not like I'll have the opportunity again."

Teasing, Gore said, "No doubt. I'm hoping to have *that* room if I ever stay over." He laughed. "I seem to recall you having the painters come back, what was it four times, when you were redoing the Georgetown house?"

Gesturing to the ceiling with hands and eyes, Jackie said, "You sound just like Jack." Now imitating Jack in a deeper register, "'Jackie, how different can beige be?'" She laughed. "Jack once asked my mother, 'Mrs. Auchincloss, do you think we're prisoners of beige?' He thinks he's so funny!"

"I think he is," Gore remarked nodding. "And what about the rest of it? It's a huge undertaking. Must be overwhelming."

Nodding yes, Jackie said, "To be honest I was appalled by the state of the mansion. I thought what impression does it give visiting heads of state? The furniture is a total mishmash. The drapery, just awful. The house needs help, but I can't do it alone."

"Who have you enlisted to help?" Gore asked, earnestly curious.

Fixing herself an oyster, Jackie said, "Bunny Mellon knows everyone!" Her eyes widening with a knowing look. "Because of her influence, really her arm twisting, she's got people donating their family heirlooms. It's incredible!" Jackie grinned. "I can't believe my luck. I'm working with the French décorator, who restored Versailles! Can you imagine? His name is Stephane Boudin. And I've got another expert who is *the* last word on American antiques, Mr. Henry DuPont. I had to fire Sister Parish. I think she slapped Caroline."

"Well, that's not good!" Gore sympathized.

"No, it wasn't. I couldn't trust her."

"Do DuPont and Boudin work well together?" Gore asked.

"Gosh no, they butt heads. There is a huge difference in their ages and their approaches. Boudin is all about esthetics while DuPont is all about authenticity. I've learned more from Boudin than I have from all the architecture books I ever read." Jackie was jazzed to be able to talk about her project.

"How do you manage it with these two?"

"I've learned to meet with them separately." Laughing, "Last week Stephane breezed through the Blue Room and eyed a round table covered with a fringed tablecloth. He ordered it gone;" she cut her hand through the air in imitation, "because he felt it made the table look like a fat Spanish dancer." Jackie laughed. "He was right!"

"Sounds a bit temperamental," observed Gore and laughed.

"Maybe," she shrugged, "but fun to work with. I even managed to find some historic furniture in government storage rooms."

"Ah, clever girl! It sounds like a regular scavenger hunt."

"It is actually." she said nodding excitedly. "I asked Mr. West, if he knew where I could find more authentic furniture and objects? He's the Chief Usher and really, he runs the place."

Mr. J.B. West was indispensable to the current First Lady as he had been to both Mamie Eisenhower and Bess Truman before her. He understood the inner workings of the mansion, how it was run and needed to be run to function smoothly for the family that currently inhabited it and as a welcoming haven for heads of state, visiting dignitaries, and invited guests of the family. She was developing a special relationship with Mr. West. As Chief Usher, he was able to anticipate her needs, often before she herself was aware of them. He recognized, underneath her controlled exterior, a free spirit, eventually becoming close enough to be able to tease her...within boundaries that she clearly set. Underneath the dignified face she showed the world, in private, she possessed an irreverent sense of humor. They both enjoyed practical jokes.

When the President was given a birthday party by staff, it was the First Lady and the Chief Usher who dug up a patch of dead crab grass from the White House lawn and presented the grass to him elegantly wrapped as a boxed present. The dead crab grass patches on the lawn perpetually perturbed the President no end.

Jack's sense of humor did not fail him at the party. Everyone enjoyed the apparent joke at his expense. Upon opening the present Jack quipped grinning, "My wife seems to have a handle on what to get the man who has everything?" There was not another person on earth whose smile could light up a room like Jack's.

Jackie's style was different from previous First Ladies. She did not adhere to a prescribed schedule. Mrs. Truman had a set time in the morning to meet with Mr. West and she would dictate her needs for the day over coffee in her sitting room. In contrast, and bordering on the bizarre, Mrs. Eisenhower took her meeting with Mr. West sitting up in her bed wearing a pink quilted bed jacket and a pink bow in her hair. The meeting was precisely at nine o'clock. Mr. West would arrive punctually with his notebook in hand. Everything on Mamie's list pertained to "the General" as she called him. His needs and his comforts were her prime concern.

On one morning, a quite frantic Mrs. Eisenhower called him at home early. Could he come as soon as possible, there was an emergency?

"Is it medical?" he asked alarmed.

"No, it isn't, but it's an emergency. You'll understand when you get here."

When Mr. West arrived at the private quarters, he knocked on the Eisenhower's bedroom door as instructed. Mamie opened the door herself and he noticed right away that her nose, especially around the nostrils, was black. The upholstered headboard had what appeared to be black fingerprints all over, so did the sheets, pillowcases, and bedspread. But that was not all, the President's bald head had black smudges, and so did his face. Sitting up in bed, he looked bewildered.

Mamie explained that during the night she had a stuffy nose and not wanting to disturb the President, she neglected to turn on the light and had confused the ink bottle with nose drops. Throughout the night she was unknowingly putting ink into her nose.

Mr. West called in a dry cleaner to take care

113

of the bed and to help the Eisenhowers remove the ink from their persons. Impossible as it may seem; it was a story that Mr. West kept strictly under wraps. If Mrs. Eisenhower wanted to share the story, he reasoned, it was hers to tell.

Part of the job of Chief Usher was discretion and Mr. West had that characteristic in spades. As much as he felt Jackie would appreciate the humor of the episode, he knew that revealing it would break a trust. A trust that the new First Lady could interpret as one easily broken with her. It was not worth the risk. She insisted on loyalty and Mr. West was only too happy to comply.

Jackie was a different First Lady in her approach. She and Mr. West did not have set meeting times. She would grab him on the fly, speak to him on a staircase or in a hallway as their paths crossed. Sometimes, when she was considering fabric samples that she had spread out on the floor, he would join her sitting on the carpet. Because of the unpredictability, he never left his office without his notebook, so he was never caught off guard.

Jackie continued, "You would be surprised to know, there are storage rooms piled from floor to ceiling, Mr. West told me no one had ever asked to go in them!" she said incredulously. "Most of it is junk," she shrugged, "but occasionally, a gem. We even found President Lincoln's dinner plates," she revealed, pleased as punch. "I use them in the private dining room because all that's left are the plates."

"Well, that is exciting!" Gore agreed, nodding. "What else have you stumbled on?"

Lowering her voice, she offered, "Thomas Jefferson's inkwell and we found George Washington's armchair on a dirt floor in what was Fort Washington on the Potomac. Of course, Washington never lived in the White House, but it is right that his chair is there."

"Who could argue with that?" Gore agreed. "Well, I must say, that is thrilling."

"Of course, Jack loves that I'm doing the restoration," she crossed her legs and adjusted herself in her chair. "He's given me carte blanche. I got the National Gallery to loan me a Monet for our living quarters and five American Indian Chief portrait paintings by George Caitlin that I've hung in the hallway on the second floor. There is also one with a buffalo that's in Jack's Oval Office. Do you know Caitlin's work? The portraits are amazing!"

"Capitalizing on the new frontier," Gore nodded, "excellent idea! Yes, marvelous paintings. I know them. I loved them as a boy. Maybe you can get one for me?" he kidded.

"Truth is, I don't think I could bear to live in that house without doing the restoration." Leaning forward with her left elbow resting on the table she grabbed a lock of her hair and twirled it absent-mindedly, "Of course, there is no money, but I have in mind to print little souvenirs books that will cost only a dollar. Nothing wrong with having a memento."

"I think it's a brilliant idea," Gore remarked agreeing, "it will certainly help with expenses."

And indeed, it would. Within a year of the restoration, one million people toured the mansion, purchased the souvenir book, and paid for the restoration.

Draining her glass, she smiled, "Mmm, that hit the spot. There is a lot about the White House that we wanted to change and not just the decor. Our style of entertaining is less formal than the Eisenhowers."

"Yes, and I'll drink to that!" Gore said, raising his glass.

Jackie rolled her eyes, "When Jack was a senator, going to the White House was just unbearable. Ike and Mamie would sit and everyone else stood. There was nothing to drink," Jackie shook her head in disbelief. "We made up our minds that nobody would be as bored as that!"

"I certainly agree that the atmosphere is so different now and there is plenty to drink," Gore smiled, remembering a party he had attended earlier in the spring. "Eliminating the receiving line, you and Jack breezing around chatting among the guests, is a stroke of genius."

"And more fun for us!"

The waiter arrived with bowls of clam chowder and packages of oyster crackers. "Would you care for another round?"

Jackie nodded.

Gore answered, "By all means. Thank you."

"Mmm, it's thick, the way I like it!" said Jackie, enjoying the chowder. "Would you please pass the pepper?"

Gore handed her the pepper before helping himself. He dropped in the small round oyster crackers that floated in the chowder. Jackie did the same.

"How did you talk Jack into ballet and classical recitals?" Gore smirked, cocking his head.

"I impressed upon him that entertainment doesn't have to be aimed at the lowest common denominator."

"And he went for it?" Gore laughed.

"I still can't believe it myself," she smirked. "It's appalling what we spend on the Pentagon and so little for the arts."

"Well, you're in an excellent position to influence."

Jackie smiled, "I think The White House should set the standard, not follow one. Jack asked the cellist, Pablo Casals to perform after a dinner we are having for the Governor of Puerto Rico. Casals is 85 now and living in Puerto Rico. He's in exile from Spain."

"Yes, I remember."

"But here's the thing. Mr. Casals is delighted to accept the invitation to perform but he won't eat dinner. He can't forgive our government recognizing Franco's Spain."

Gore put down his spoon, "Jack, I imagine, respects Casals's principles and his frankness."

"Yes," Jackie agreed, "Jack thinks a man is nothing without his ideals."

"That is true."

Continuing, Jackie added, "This will be Casals second time at the White House. The first time was in 1904 when Teddy Roosevelt was in office. Roosevelt's daughter, Alice, is coming. She was at the first concert."

"Was she?" Gore marveled, "Your attention to detail is astonishing! How many people would think to invite Teddy Roosevelt's daughter sixty years later?"

The waiter delivered two gin and tonics.

Jackie smiled and nodded. "We're also inviting the singer, Harry Belafonte and two American composers, Aaron Copeland and Leonard Bernstein."

"Those three would be interesting to have at your table."

"I've thought about that." She sipped her drink. "Remember, I must save some interesting people for Jack's table too."

"When you think I'm relevant for a certain evening's theme, I'll clear my dance card. Incidentally, be sure to put Alice at Jack's table. She'll keep the conversation lively, she's absolutely vicious."

"Thanks for the tip. We have you in mind for future dinners. I wasn't jumping on the 'vicious' just then, I swear. Just so you know."

"That's a relief," Gore said, and they both laughed. "Tell me above all else, what's the best thing about being in the White House?"

"I can give you two. Fresh flowers every day and fresh sheets twice a day." She said with a Mona

Lisa-like smile.

"Hmm...fresh sheets twice a day. I can't think why!" Gore laughed.

"I can tell you the worst part was training the staff, especially the younger maids who work for us in the private quarters. I had to find a way to get the staff to stop being so afraid of me."

There were two young maids, in particular, who were part of the staff that Jackie saw qualities she was looking for. She wanted someone who could anticipate a guests' needs and would be comfortable enough to be friendly without being familiar, if only she could get them to calm down. This was the South after all, with charming ways of hospitality, but her ways were different. Still, she wanted visiting guests to feel at ease and the right person in the role could make a big difference.

"Who could be afraid of little old you?" Gore mocked.

Dressed to the Nines

"How's your summer been?" Gore asked.

"Relaxing. Big lunches on the sailboat every weekend. Jack's in his glory and it's good for the children to be with their cousins."

"Even though Bobby's kids are a bit wild."

Smiling and nudging Gore off handedly, Jackie offered, "Ethel does have her hands full." Continuing, Jackie explained, "While everyone is on the lawn killing themselves with touch football, Jack's father and I discuss all sorts of things: history, current events, books. His Hollywood stories are quite compelling."

Jackie finished her bowl of chowder and placed her spoon in the empty bowl.

"You know Jack met Gloria Swanson when he was a boy. At that time, Gloria was the most famous woman in the world."

"Did Jack meet her in Hollywood?" Gore asked.

"No," Jackie said shaking her head, "His father brought Gloria home to have dinner with the family."

Raising an eyebrow, Gore offered, "Rose must have been thrilled!"

Smiling and giving a knowing look, "Oh, Rose wasn't home. She was in Paris shopping for her fall wardrobe."

Gore nodded, "Jack doesn't expect you to interact with his siblings?"

"Let me put it this way; one of the first times I played touch football with them I broke my ankle. After that, I was off the hook."

"Quite a price to pay, I'd say!" Gore leaned back; one arm slung over the back of his chair. He crossed his legs, letting a bare ankle rest on his knee.

Smiling and shrugging, "Jack's sisters had never seen the likes of anyone resembling me before. The very first time I was invited to Hyannis Port for the weekend, I wore these Roman toga sandals with straps that crisscrossed all the way up my calf. One look at me and they decided I was a pretentious snob," she laughed.

Gore smirked, "They obviously expected Jack to be with a different kind of woman. Someone more *like* them. The unforgivable sin was being different. But" Gore lifted an index finger for emphasis, "I think that's just the thing that made you attractive to Jack."

Jackie nodded, "My first dinner with his

family, I came down dressed to the nines. Perhaps I over did it, but my family always dressed for dinner; and I wanted to make a good impression. Jack took one look at me and said, "Where do you think *you're* going?'"

"Ouch!"

"He really hurt my feelings, but his mother came to my rescue. I didn't know what to expect but I'll tell you what I was not prepared for, was Jack's sisters bursting into my room without knocking. Can you imagine?" Jackie shook her head, "At dinner, they flung scorching insults toward one another. I felt like I was being interrogated. Thank God, I had read Hemingway and saw *Singin' in the Rain*, that seemed to be the extent of their cultural intellect."

Gore laughed.

"I surprised myself how I got up the nerve to stand up to them including Jack's father. But I did. Everything was a test," She shrugged. "Of course, I was intimidated, the environment I grew up in was almost still by comparison.... once Daddy moved out. I missed him but at least there was no more shouting. At home at the dinner table, there was polite conversation. Mummy critiqued table manners, and kept tabs on school, who our friends were, and what we were involved in. But Daddy was completely the opposite knowing how strict and inflexible our mother was, he made sure that we only had fun with him."

"Well, that's a nice balance," Gore offered, "but I imagine it must have had a destabilizing effect."

Jackie cocked her head, "Yes, I think you are right about that." She was wistful for a moment. "I was his favorite."

"How could you not be, you looked just like him!" Jackie smiled,

"Yes, well, Mummy favored Lee. Parents are not supposed to have favorites, but they didn't hide their feelings," she shrugged.

Jackie was a member of another family now and she found her place in it but on her terms. It helped considerably that she had forged a friendship with Jack's father. It was a mutual admiration society between the two of them. Even Jack had remarked on it, and it pleased him.

Jack's father understood, that in life, image was everything and particularly in politics. It was Joe Kennedy who introduced Jackie to his friend, the American clothing designer, Oleg Cassini. Mr. Cassini distinguished himself as the only designer who showed her wardrobe sketches particularly for her and specifically for her role as First Lady.

The two other designers, who had also come to see her in the hospital after she had given birth to baby John, showed her dresses from their current collections. She did not want that. For her, it was of the utmost importance that no one else have her dresses. Cassini promised that. The clothes he would make would be for her alone. He impressed her. Not only did he have pedigree, born to an aristocratic Russian family with Italian ancestry on his mother's side, he was handsome and dressed impeccably; something she wished for her own husband. When she first met Jack, his style was rumpled Ivy League. She persuaded Jack to have tailored suits made that hung more attractively on his lean physique.

It was Oleg Cassini who presented her with the idea that she, as First Lady would be playing a role for which she must dress the part. The idea had great appeal. Suddenly, she saw herself as one of her admired French heroines. The collaboration was set. She and Mr. Cassini would work together, and, in that realm, they forged a lasting friendship.

Her father-in-law was one of the wealthiest men in America and in a position to be generous. It was his pleasure to contribute in this way. None of them knew exactly what all this would cost. She agreed, image was everything. And so, the bargain was made, Jack's father would be sent the bills and pay for all of it. There was no argument. The only glaring obstacle was making sure the press never got wind of the astronomically mounting tally.

"Apparently you passed...with flying colors," Gore smiled.

Khrushchev's Puppy

The waiter brought the mussels and linguini.

"Thanks very much," Jackie said.

Digging into her linguini, "Mmm, this is yummy!"

"So how did Jack propose? Did he get down on one knee?" Gore asked.

Jackie laughed, "We weren't even in the same country let alone the same room. I was in London covering Queen Elizabeth's coronation for my column in *The Times-Herald* staying in a flat in Mayfair that had no heat. A cablegram arrived with a message from Jack asking if I'd marry him?"

"How romantic! — Is it romantic? I honestly don't know." Gore asked baffled. "And did you answer right away?"

"No," she shook her head and smiled. "I was with a girlfriend. After we finished our work in London, we went to Paris for ten days. During the day, Aileen and I visited museums. The whole time I thought about nothing else but Jack's proposal. Although in the evenings, I got dressed up and went out with my old beau, Jack Marquand. He had been the man I was seeing in Paris when I lived there for six months. I was crazy about him."

Gore smiled, "You sly little minx! When did you finally give Jack your answer?"

"When I came home, and Jack met my plane. I came out of customs and there was Jack standing by a counter."

"I'd say that *is* romantic. Bravo!"

"Gosh, yes, I thought it was romantic at the time. It's ancient history now." She shrugged and expertly twirled her linguini.

"Did Jack present you with that eye-smacking ring at the airport?"

Jackie laughed. "No. That came later."

Once the engagement was secured, it was Jack's father, who paid a visit to the exclusive French jeweler, Louis Van Cleef at the beautifully appointed Manhattan Van Cleef & Arpels Fifth Avenue location. Kennedy and Van Cleef's friendship spanned decades. It was Louis's wife, Helene, who accompanied Rose Kennedy to the Paris couture fashion houses and selected her clothes. Helene Van Cleef was on the *Best Dressed List* for an entire decade. She had it all, a beautiful face, a striking figure, good taste, and staggering wealth.

Selecting jewelry was just the sort of assignment Joe Kennedy relished and just the sort that bored his son to tears. Jack, having no patience for sentimentality, was able to hide his shortcoming because his father was only too happy to come to the rescue. When it came to women Joe possessed great instincts, and a certain feel for what suited them specifically, when it came to choosing finery and the perfect piece.

Louis Van Cleef, himself, greeted Joe Kennedy at his salon's front entrance and escorted him to a private sitting room, decorated with walls covered in charcoal-colored silk damask, cream-colored paneling, and magnificent over-sized crystal chandeliers. Coffee was served in a beautiful service. It was in this relaxed and esthetically pleasing atmosphere that Louis Van Cleef asked his friend if he had brought a picture of the young lady? The response was no. It did not matter, Mr. Van Cleef had done his homework. He knew she was young with sophisticated tastes.

Joe Kennedy was brought three pieces of jewelry to examine and consider. The first, a ring with two three-carat emerald cut stones, had a white diamond and a deep green emerald. Each were surrounded in a swirl of diamond and emerald baguettes. It was a showstopper. The other pieces were a diamond and ruby bracelet meant as a wedding present to Jackie from Jack, and the third piece, a diamond encrusted pin in the shape of a leaf. Later, Jack presented the pin as a present to Jackie after Caroline's birth. Joe asked that all three pieces be sent to his Hyannis Port residence. He never asked the price of any of the items, and none were offered.

"Do you know Khrushchev sent the children a puppy?" Jackie grinned.

"Has this one been up in space?" Gore asked.

"No, but the mother has."

"I believe that dog's name is Strelka, right?" Gore offered.

"Is there anything you don't remember?" Jackie was genuinely impressed.

"It can be a curse, but more often than not, it's a useful trait."

"In Vienna, Mr. Khrushchev tried to impress me that the schools in the Soviet Union were the best in the world. I said to him, 'Please, Mr. Chairman, don't bore me with statistics.' I think my comment surprised and amused him," Jackie said, pleased with herself.

"I imagine he was surprised." Gore laughed, impressed.

Jackie continued, "If he had said that their caviar was the best in the world, now that I would believe!" They both laughed.

"I was running out of conversation, so I asked about the dog the Soviets had sent up into space and asked him for a puppy. I was surprised he sent it!"

Gore shook his head affirmatively, "You have a way of getting what you want. What did Jack say about the puppy?"

"I can't remember. Probably, 'Christ, another dog!'"

"You should have asked for one of those fabulous Faberge eggs?"

Jackie snapped her head and sat back in her chair, "What a blunder. That was stupid of me!" She laughed. Not missing a beat, she recovered, "You know when we met, Khrushchev insisted on shaking my hand before Jack's." Self-satisfied, Jackie sipped her cocktail.

"Well, that isn't difficult to understand, Mrs. Khrushchev resembles a potato."

As she was in mid sip, Jackie nearly choked. "You are terrible!" Recovering, "Okay, she looks like a farmer's wife, I concede." Leaning in, "Mrs. Khrushchev looks sweet, but President de Gaulle warned me that she is sneakier than Nikita."

Pulling a mussel from its shell with her fork, Jackie mused, "I imagine it's a dreadful place to live. I would love to see the colorful onion domes in Red Square."

"The Russians refer to those domes as turnips," Gore offered.

"How interesting," Jackie mused, "And naturally, I would love to visit the Hermitage Museum. Have you been?"

"No, but it is on my list, of course!" Gore dabbed his mouth and replaced the napkin in his lap.

"Well, you certainly charmed de Gaulle. Jack told me you dazzled him at the Versailles dinner." Gore twirled and ate some linguini. "What a fantastic spectacle! The French were certainly crazy about you."

Jackie smiled twirling the long tendrils without splashing, "France did go well. Jack was so pleased," she nearly purred. "I had written to de Gaulle before the trip. I wanted him to know how much I love French history and culture. I suggested to Jack that he read de Gaulle's memoirs, so he'd have a sense of the whole man. I think it really helped forge a friendship between our two countries." She leaned in, "That dinner at Versailles was magical, the shimmer of the chandeliers, the candlelight."

"The sparkle from all the heirloom jewelry must have been blinding."

Jackie laughed, "You're right; it was blinding. I borrowed the most marvelous diamond brooches from Van Cleef & Arpels, and my hairdresser put them in my hair. The press said it was a tiara, but I wouldn't have done that."

"And yet, the effect was the same. Dazzling!"

"One works with what one has," she smiled.

There were two magical evenings in Paris on that trip in which she would conjure from memory and bask. The first and other dinner located in the heart of Paris was held in the 18th century magnificence of the Elysée Palace, built by King Louis XV for his mistress, Madame Pompadour. Used now as the residence for the President of France, de Gaulle was only too happy to host a dinner for JFK and the thrilled Mrs. Kennedy. Three hundred guests enjoyed a dinner using Napoleon's vermeil flatware and Sèvres porcelain, the kind of dinnerware she had only seen in museums.

Jack was handsome in white-tie and tails. Jackie's pink and white raffia lace gown designed by Oleg Cassini had the desired effect, adoration. The dress, elegant in its simplicity, contrasted with her hair elaborately done with sultry bangs that swept her forehead and nearly obscured her right eye, the rest of her hair sculpted in a variation of a modified Geisha's wig. Diana Vreeland, editor of *Harper's Bazaar*, and arbiter of taste and style had suggested the fabric for the gown which, woven from straw, was light as a feather. It is a wonder Jackie did not float away. She felt she was walking on air the entire evening.

It was a fortuitous opportunity to see some of the salons in the Elysée Palace which she considered the epitome of French architectural grace and splendor, each room different from the next. The painted paneling in the rooms, finished so precisely and gilded with gold leaf, the painted ceilings depicting nature, nymphs, flowers, and mythological characters complimented with perfectly proportioned furniture, and shimmering chandeliers in each room made her heart sing. She hoped to bring some of the same exquisite style to the White House.

As if the dinner at Elysée Palace could not be topped, Jackie and JFK were honored with another dinner the following evening at the Palace of Versailles, built by Louis XIV as his primary residence in 1682. To be at Versailles, dining by candlelight in the famous Hall of Mirrors was a thing of dreams. To have a candlelight dinner, in her honor, was beyond imagination, yet it had been real, and Jackie was determined to savor every moment. As she walked through the palace, she was more than aware that it was Louis XIV's vision that she was experiencing. Louis XIV, also known as the Sun King, was the person who had worked personally with the architects that made the palace possible. It was Louis XIV who commissioned the artists who painted the murals and the paintings of Versailles. It was Louis XIV who approved or dismissed a plan for the gardens which took decades to execute. It was all here, just as Louis XIV envisioned it; still standing, still gleaming, and still admired nearly three hundred years later.

  These facts were swimming in her mind as she glided through the palace on the arm of President de Gaulle. When they arrived at The Hall of Mirrors bathed in candlelight and festooned with stunning over-sized floral arrangements, she was breathless. Ecstatic to be at Versailles under these auspicious circumstances, she was ever grateful to her sister, Lee for personally working with Mr. Hubert Givenchy to make the most sublime gown for the occasion. In the dress, Jackie presented herself as the paradigm of French elegance.

The gown was ivory silk with a sleeveless fitted bodice of embroidered flowers in muted tones, which mirrored in a way the elegant vests men wore under their jackets in Louis XIV's court. A matching floor length, ivory silk evening coat was so simple in form and design it resembled a Japanese kimono. This time her hair was swept away from her face and elaborately piled on her head. All the easier to see every detail by which to imprint her memory with no impediment.

If she did not pinch herself literally, again and again, she made mental notes. This is really happening. I am here. The only person she felt would understand her true feelings was her sister to which the two compared their shared experience in rapturous minute detail.

Defying Gravity

Gore sat back in his chair and briefly surveyed the room. The dining room was filling up but as luck would have it, they had no diners immediately next to them. It was still early for dinner, for them it was really a late lunch. Still, he had wondered if their waiter tipped off the manager who then instructed the staff to give them a wide berth.

Jackie announced she needed to powder her nose. Gore stood, pulled out her chair, and pointed her in the right direction. Jackie was adept at finding her way nonchalantly without meeting anyone's gaze. Clint, upon seeing her leave the table, casually left his seat at the bar, and walked to where the Ladies and Gents facilities were located. He waited patiently nearby monitoring who entered and exited. While Jackie was gone, Gore signaled the waiter for another round.

Jackie traversed a darkish hallway but easily found a four paneled door painted glossy-white with a small black sign marked "Ladies." She turned the wood doorknob and entered an empty washroom. A wooden table had a nice touch, a vase of fresh sunflowers.

She entered the last of four stalls. Being alone did not last long. The stall beside hers became occupied. After several seconds she heard, "Oh, great! There's no paper."

"I can spare some," Jackie offered and gathered a generous length of paper that she rolled around her hand and slipped under the partition.

"Thanks, you're a lifesaver."

"Don't mention it." Jackie flushed, opened the stall door, and noticed extra toilet rolls on the table. She grabbed one and offered it under the door of the stall, "Here's a roll for you."

"Thanks, again."

Jackie stood before one of two sinks. There was no place to put her purse, so she placed it on the wooden table. The soap dispenser had granular *Boraxo* but at least the dispenser was full. She wet her hands, pushed the lever, and got a tiny pyramid amount in her palm and scrubbed her hands. After rinsing, she used paper towels. The electric dryer, she reasoned, would take too long. She opened her purse and took out her lipstick and applied a fresh coat all the way to the corners by making an "O" with her mouth. It was a trick Diana Vreeland had passed on that she claimed, made the mouth look less "painted." She ran her fingers through her hair and smoothed out her blouse.

The third stall door opened, and the occupant went straight for the other sink. Intent on getting soap, she hardly noticed Jackie. When she did look up, she got a glimpse of her in the mirror, just as Jackie was turning to open the door to leave.

"Thanks again for the T.P.," said the woman, "Hey, you look just like..."

Opening the door while exiting, Jackie breezily answered on her way out, "Funny, I don't see it!"

Gore watched Jackie appear first and then Clint at a short distance following. The short procession parted and as Jackie approached the table, Gore rose and pulled out her chair.

"All well?"

"I managed to not fall in," she smiled.

"I took the liberty of ordering us another round," Gore said, pointing out the cocktail to her. "Would you care for dessert?" Gore asked.

"I wouldn't say no to strawberry shortcake."

"Excellent idea," Gore smiled, and got the waiter's attention.

"Sir, something else?"

"Yes, how's the strawberry short cake?" Gore inquired.

"Homemade fresh with farm stand strawberries, it's very good," the waiter replied, knowing how to sell it.

"Great," said Gore, "We'll each have one, and please one more for my friend in the green shirt sitting at the bar."

"Very good, sir," came the answer and with that the waiter turned on his heel and headed for the kitchen.

Dessert settled, Gore fiddling with a straw smiled and asked, "How are your mother and Uncle Hugh, or does he prefer, Unk?"

Jackie smirked; her tongue slid inside of her cheek as she assessed where Gore might be going, her eyebrows raised. Both elbows on the table, she cradled her face resting two closed hands on either side of her chin. "Oh, I think you know the answer."

Gore was not finished with the set up by any stretch, "Unk's a man who enjoys great wealth without hesitation or vulgarity. It's what drew our mothers to him. Frankly, there isn't much else to draw on," Gore winked at her. "Once she laid eyes on it, Merrywood, that is, was a determining factor, for *my* mother. Tennis courts, stables, lush gardens, swimming pools!" Gore spread his hands like fans for emphasis, "But in one way or another, we try to recreate that heavenly ambiance in our own households."

Jackie smiled and rolled her eyes. "How old

were you when you moved into Merrywood?" Jackie asked, curiously trying to piece the time frame together. She sipped her drink.

"I was ten." Gore answered.

As it happened, shortly after Gore's mother divorced his father, Nina Gore, became the second wife of one, Hugh D. Auchincloss, of the Standard Oil fortune, member of the Social Register, and a Wall Street stockbroker. Auchincloss was swimming in money, just the kind Gore's mother hoped to get her hands on.

Her contribution to the union was youth and beauty. Auchincloss was impotent. Nina figured wrongly that sexual relations would not figure into the bargain. Uncle Hugh had other ideas. Somehow, she managed to produce two offspring for him.

"Did you know Unk is impotent?" he asked her pointedly.

Jackie, mid sip nearly spewed across the table caught herself and wide eyed, replied, "No, apparently Mummy forgot to tell me." She broke into laughter.

"He's no swordsman that's for sure," Gore delighted in offering.

"I didn't suspect he was Errol Flynn in the sack," Jackie was in hysterics, barely able to get the

141

remark out.

Gore then spilled what he had been saving for last, "My mother told me that she collected Unk's sperm with a spoon to manage the job."

Now they were both in hysterics.

There was not much that Gore found interesting about Uncle Hugh other than his vast pornography collection. Children have a way of discovering secrets and hiding places.

"No wonder that both our mothers named our half-sisters after themselves. I guess they thought they had earned *that* honor by defying gravity and all." Gore mused, "My mother must have hung upside down until she was dizzy." He laughed. "Having a child with Hugh was surely an insurance policy for her future solvency."

"Great, now how will I be able to ever look Uncle Hugh in the eye again? Gee, thanks!" Jackie remarked incredulously.

Gore relished going over their shared history, their connection by marriage. "Wait 'til Jack finds out." Gore smirked, pleased with himself as he dabbed his mouth with his napkin. "They do have one thing in common as I think about it. Trouble! Your mother makes trouble, mine *is* trouble!"

"Mummy can be difficult," Jackie agreed. "Less so now, *not* that she's changed... *but I have.*"

Gore had a story to illustrate his relationship, or lack thereof, with Jackie's mother.

"I don't think I told you about the time I was invited back to Merrywood after a fifteen-year absence at my half-sister Nini's insistence. She was nineteen at the time. Now I was a famous writer and Nini was in awe." Gore paused to sip his cocktail. "Apparently, your mother wasn't keen on the idea of having me, but she more or less complied. There wasn't enough room at the big table at lunch, so, she set up a card table for four and stuck me with eight and ten-year-olds."

"How egalitarian of her!" Jackie laughed, wide-eyed and shaking her head.

"I fixed her. Within minutes of the start of the meal, I had my dinner companions roaring with laughter. It completely killed any conversation at the big table because all the adults were dying to know what we were talking about. Of course, your mother never forgave me," Gore smirked.

Jackie laughed, "That's one lunch I'm sorry I missed."

"Nini, was *always* a smart kid. I give her credit for leaving our mother when she was just thirteen to go live with her father and your mother. I'll say this, your mother may be many things but one thing she is not, is alcoholic. I know for a fact your mother was fair in her treatment of her. I am grateful for that." Then adding thoughtfully, Gore asked, "At what age were you when your mother married Uncle Hugh?"

"I was just thirteen and Lee nine when we moved into Merrywood."

There was no crossover between Jackie and Gore living at the same time in Merrywood, a grand estate, located in a suburb of Washington. By that time, Gore was in the Army. He had left Merrywood upon his mother and Auchincloss's divorce when he was sixteen. During the school year, he had been in one boarding school or another and had spent only six summers with Uncle Hugh. Some of that time was spent with his own father and his maternal grandparents, all of whom he adored.

When Nini moved into Merrywood with her father and Jackie's mother, Jackie was twenty-one and out on her own. It was a complicated business and having some of this shared family drama was interesting to them both.

"Of course, my mother had insatiable appetites. She was very indiscriminate when it came to sex and booze." Gore smiled wickedly.

"Yes, as you mentioned!" Jackie exclaimed.

"Thankfully, I lived in Washington with my grandparents for most of my childhood. My grandfather, Senator Gore, I don't think I told you, was blind from childhood from two very unfortunate accidents that each took an eye. As I recall, he was very patient as I sounded out all the big words. I read fascinating passages like upcoming legislation and issues of the day." Gore laughed. "Naturally, at age five, I hadn't a clue what any of it meant."

As a young boy, Gore Vidal often accompanied his grandfather to the Senate floor, thereby obtaining a first-hand grasp of political maneuvering.

"Remarkable. Blind from childhood," Jackie was fascinated. "I was also reading at the age of five," she thought he'd be interested knowing, "I could recite from memory passages of *The Wonderful Wizard of Oz* and *Winnie-the-Pooh*. My mother told me I picked up a Chekov novel but when I asked her what the word "midwife" meant she took the book away. It was back to *Little Lord Fauntleroy.*" Jackie laughed.

"It was *Arabian Nights* for me, Jules Verne, and *The Three Musketeers*. My grandfather's library was enormous. He once had to fire a maid who got the bright idea of rearranging all the books by color. After that, he couldn't find anything and neither could anyone else," he laughed.

Pulling a cigarette from her purse, she put it to her lips, Gore lit it for her. Jackie exhaled, "What about your mother? Did she live with you?"

"On and off. My mother was like an evil spirit that came into a room. That was her mother's description of her! My father was an engineer and involved in aeronautics. You know, in the '30s he founded three different airlines."

"That's impressive," Jackie agreed.

"My father thought within a decade or so, everyone would have his or her own private planes, like we all have our own cars. Can you imagine had that happened?"

"No, thank heaven it didn't happen."

"You know, as a boy I knew Amelia Earhart. She was a very close friend of my father's."

"How amazing!" Jackie exclaimed.

"Yes. She was fearless!" Gore offered, then added, "That probably goes without saying."

Jackie already engrossed, perked up.

Gore's voice dropped a bit and he added thoughtfully, "When she disappeared, I was devastated. They said she must have run out of fuel, but she was too smart for that." He paused to look Jackie in the eye, "As I reflect on it now, I believe she found a small, secluded island to spend the rest of her life. In a loveless marriage, she wanted out," nodding, "yes, I do believe it was deliberate."

Jackie chewed her fingernail while she absorbed this rather startling information. "But her plane crashed! They never found her or the wreckage."

"That's true, they never did. Still, I have this hunch and I think I am right. I don't think she ran out of fuel like they said." Gore was convinced.

"Just when you'd imagine Amelia Earhart not fascinating enough!" Jackie remarked in awe.

"My father thought showing a ten-year-old kid flying and landing a plane would promote the idea of everyone having one. As a kid, I lived for Mickey Rooney and the movies. Rooney was my hero. When the cameras rolled, I must have imagined myself, as him. It was horrifying to see it was just me looking into the camera and explaining what it was like to fly. Remember, this was the Depression. The timing could not have been worse for such a highfalutin idea."

The ice made a tinkling sound as Jackie and Gore sipped their drinks.

147

"I know what you mean about seeing yourself in newsreels, it is horrible!" Jackie confessed.

"It is difficult seeing yourself, especially *as the spectacle* you've become," Gore said when Jackie interrupted.

"Gee thanks!"

"No," Gore smiled, "*You* aren't a spectacle, your popularity makes you the spectacle. That's what I am trying to say, rather clumsily," he shrugged.

"Golly, maybe I'll never leave my bedroom. Some days I feel like that."

"Don't we all!" Gore said.

"When I was younger, I had imagined, no fantasized about my French heroines, women I admired, like Madame Récamier. She had those 19th century French Salon evenings in Paris with the great minds of the day. She was intelligent and glamorous, the toast of Paris, and modern for the time. It's exactly what I imagined for myself, evenings bringing together great minds for ideas and conversation." Jackie had one arm on the table, the other arm holding the back of her neck as she rested an elbow on the back of her chair.

Gore offered, "Well, by Jove, I think you've done it! You have fashioned yourself as a modern embodiment. Don't tell me you didn't fancy yourself Marie Antoinette at that dinner at Versailles or at the very least, imagined her there?"

"I'm not sure I like the metaphor," Jackie smiled, "she came to a bad end. I think, I'll stick with Madame Récamier for inspiration." Jackie stubbed out her cigarette.

"Do you think women like Nefertiti and Cleopatra were copied in their time?" Gore asked.

"Without question, I think so," Jackie said with enthusiasm. "Simply look at the art created by the Ancient Egyptians. It brings us into their highly formed, aesthetic world. I am certain they weren't the first women to be admired but they gave us a treasure trove of evidence that they were, and if not worshipped, certainly adored."

Gore confessed, "I feel rather silly admitting this, but it took me awhile to realize Renaissance painters were painting their subjects in clothing and finery of *their* day, even when they were depicting Biblical themes."

Jackie laughed. "But isn't it fun when you stumble upon a revelation?"

Gore nodded, agreeing. "Inspiration *is* what we desire to give dimension to our lives," he finished.

"It's the reason for travel, for reading books,

all aspects of life have to be explored," Jackie said.

"Ah, yes," Gore agreed, "and of course, writing books!"

Jackie said, "Certainly writing, in your case. I want our children to know the world and its possibilities." Jackie smiled, "I spend as much time with them as possible. They don't know that their lives are anything out of the ordinary. Most mornings, Caroline eats her breakfast with Jack. I'm still in bed. It's their time together. Then she walks her daddy to his office. Jack gets such a kick out of the ritual. I think part of the reason Caroline likes to go is so she can eat a piece of candy that Jack's secretary keeps on her desk."

The waiter cleared the dishes and replenished the water glasses.

Jackie waited until the waiter left them and acknowledged earnestly, "I adored my father. I could do no wrong in his eyes. My parents hated each other vehemently. They pitted me and my sister against the other parent. It was a torment. It left me terrified and terribly unsettled. Books were a great comfort to me."

"We have that in common," Gore sided with her.

"The joy on Jack's face when he's with our children makes me so happy. You know Jack fell in love with Caroline at first sight. He thought she was the prettiest baby he'd ever seen," Jackie smiled her face brightened at the memory. "At the hospital, when Caroline was born, Jack asked one of his best friends to point to the most beautiful baby in the nursery. When he pointed to the wrong one, Jack didn't speak to him for two days!" Jackie laughed.

"When I won that writing competition while I was at Vassar, the prize was a junior editor's job for *Vogue*. It meant six months in Paris and six months in New York. It was Paris, I think, that concerned my mother. She thought I'd become an expatriate, and I suppose I might have."

"Yes, I think that's exactly what she imagined. Once you had lived in Paris on your own, what on earth was going to make you return? Fortunate that you listened to her. Otherwise, she wouldn't have realized her dream of being the First Lady's mother!" Gore cracked.

"Oh you! I hate that awful term. First Lady sounds like a prized horse."

"I don't think so."

Jackie pulled out another cigarette. Gore lit it for her with a snap of his wrist.

"My mother was quite shrewd, now that I think about it. She appealed to my insecurities. She said that I wasn't sophisticated enough to work in

Paris. That I would make a fool of myself. Any confidence I had, what little I had, she stripped away."

"The tables *have* turned," Gore cocked his head.

Smiling she continued, "I turned down the prize. I can't decide if I regret it or not. I still subscribe to *French Vogue*. The press hasn't picked up on that yet!" She smirked. "In my high school yearbook, I wrote my ambition was not to be a housewife. Look at me now!"

"What a twist of fate. Still, you must admit you are probably the most famous housewife on earth! Who doesn't want to be you?"

"Well, for a while, me. When I first got married, it was terrifying," she said. Gore arched his eyebrows with a smirk on his face.

"No, not that, silly!" Jackie gave his arm a jab. "We hadn't been married that long and Jack called to tell me he invited forty senators to lunch. I had two hours to get it together. I dashed to a Greek restaurant around the corner and had forty servings of casserole and salad sent over. After that I realized, I can do this!"

"That was certainly enterprising on your part." Gore congratulated her. "My mother hated the fact that I'm homosexual. For her, this was a defect and a personal reflection on her, which is ridiculous. I'm thinking of divorcing her."

"You can't do that," Jackie said, admonishingly, "Can you?"

"I'm giving it serious thought. After all, she needs me more than I need her. Fortunately, I have always been my own person. Even as a kid, I had a strong sense of self. I never thought my parents' problems had anything to do with me."

"You are lucky to feel that way. Not everyone does," Jackie considered.

Gore shrugged it off, "You know my real name is Eugene Luther Gore Vidal. In high school at St. Alban's, I dropped the two first names because I decided at that point that I was going to be a writer. Even then I realized at the back of my mind that I didn't want to be in competition with Eugene O'Neill. How obnoxious I must have been!" Gore laughed.

"We were lucky to know ourselves even in adolescence. Our upbringings were privileged, but the challenges we faced shaped us perhaps earlier than what might be considered normal," Jackie said.

"I think that's true," Gore agreed. "I read voraciously at school, not my schoolbooks... they bored me silly. My friends at Exeter all went on to Ivy League universities: Harvard, Yale, Brown,

Princeton. School never interested me. It may surprise you to know that I got terrible grades. However, what I did learn at Exeter was honing my skills as a debater and I made quite a reputation for myself." Lifting an eyebrow, Gore added, "I was conservative then, can you image?"

Shaking her head, sipping her gin and tonic, then dragging on her cigarette and exhaling, she said, "Really, I can't."

"Immediately after high school, I enlisted in the Army. My father generously offered me my own room in his apartment in Manhattan, but his second wife was expecting their second child, and I really didn't want to be in the way. After all my mother put him through, I thought my father deserved some happiness."

Jackie nodded, "I can understand that. You must have hated school to instead join the Army?"

"It was a reflexive action. Pearl Harbor had just been bombed so I joined up, like a lot of guys my age."

"Still, it was quite brave to join especially during war time, bullets whizzing past your head."

"I was stateside ordering supplies and typing in an office. If bullets were whizzing by my head *that* would have been a serious problem!" Gore raised his eyebrows.

Jackie laughed. "How did you get that assignment? Weren't you disappointed not seeing any action?"

"My father must have pulled some strings or simply dumb luck," Gore shrugged. "Men *say* they want to see action, probably are convinced they do, but when it's actually happening, you can bet they wish it weren't."

They were quiet for a bit then Gore asked, "Who was it who said, 'There are no unwounded soldiers?'"

"Not Hemingway!" Jackie said and Gore laughed. Sitting back in her chair and crossing her legs and arms across her chest, she asked, "Did you know when my mother married Uncle Hugh, I took your old room at Merrywood?"

"No, I don't think I realized that."

"Well, I did. When I moved in, I found some of your old shirts in your closet with your name sewn in them. I used to wear them for riding. Funny how small that room was."

"That room was more like a closet. It was as good as any from which to emerge," he winked at her. "Speaking of closets and emerging from one, Tennessee arrives tomorrow."

Just then, the strawberry shortcakes arrived.

155

Mufflers & Elevators

*F*rom his vantage point, Clint Hill never let his guard down as he watched the activity in the restaurant and kept his eye on Jackie and Gore. He was careful to be discreet, not wanting to draw unnecessary attention to them. It was a delicate balance. He politely discouraged small talk from fellow customers at the bar. He was glad to see that he was not the only diner eating at the bar. But possibly, he was the only one drinking Cokes when his meal was finished.

On the job, Hill spent much of his time with the First Lady which meant all his working hours when she was out and about. When he was first assigned to her detail, she was pregnant but still wanted to take her morning walks; and he accompanied her. They walked along the Potomac River where there were few people. She initiated conversation or did not. As he was getting to know her, it was fascinating for him to see the many facets of her personality, how she could so easily converse with a queen, or mingle with heads of state, instruct painters and carpenters, determine a state dinner menu and guest list, and remember the names of White House staff workers, of which there was a considerable number, and seemed to do it all effortlessly. He noticed that she was very exacting of how she wanted things done, jobs performed and how she relied on others to make her wishes known. Everyone wanted to please her. He could see why.

She was forceful but in a quiet way. Her determination was steely, but her manner was soft. "Do you think we could possibly...?" might sound like there was some wiggle room, but when it came down to it, there was none. Even though she expected nothing but the best, she was adamant that the staff, especially the maids and housekeepers, take their vacations and have time off.

When she disagreed with her expert advisors in decorating, like Mr. DuPont, who insisted that certain objects and styles not be mixed, she would agree with him to a point, allow him to rearrange and move a painting from one place to another; but after he was gone, she would move everything back to the way she preferred. Upon Mr. DuPont's return, she was certain he noticed, but he said nothing.

Watching her from his place at the bar, Hill

observed how easily she held her own with an intellectual and well-known writer. It was nice to see her enjoying herself. She had a wonderful way of living in the moment.

"Tennessee Williams is coming here?" Jackie asked.

"The one and only!" Gore smiled and nodded.

"What a pity, I'd have loved seeing him. You must bring him to the White House."

"Yes, I will, that's a grand idea. Tennessee is the most charming man alive and the greatest company on earth. I never laugh harder with anyone. His sense of humor is wild and grotesque like mine. My pet name for him is Bird. I can't really remember why I came to call him that. Maybe because of his play, *Sweet Bird of Youth*. He calls me 'Blood and Gore'."

"Oh, charming!" Jackie laughed. "How long have you been friends?"

"We met in '48 in Rome. Italy was a terrible mess after the war. I had sailed into Naples and was shocked at how bombed out the city still was. I stayed only a few days and moved on to Rome. I remember I kept changing hotels trying to find one that had heat."

"Yes, I know what you mean; my experience

was similar. I was in London in '48 on a college trip with my Latin professor. It was disturbing to see just how bombed out London was. There were old people living under bridges. We'd never seen anything like it. What a relief it was to get to Paris and see it untouched in all its glory."

Nodding in agreement, he continued, "Paris was to be Hitler's jewel. That's the only reason he didn't bomb it. In Rome, I met Tennessee at a party, and we hit it off. Somehow, he got hold of a Jeep that had a bad muffler. It made a terrible roar, which was just as well, as Tennessee is practically blind in one eye and a horrible driver. People could hear us coming and get themselves to safety. It's a miracle he didn't kill anyone, let alone us. We moved on and terrorized the Amalfi Coast." Gore laughed. "The Italians were gorgeous. All one had to do was make eye contact with a man. So less exhausting and even the polizia looked the other way."

Captivated, Jackie listened and sipped her drink.

"I don't think I have ever been happier than I was in those days in Italy. Tennessee and I shared rooms together in Rome not to mention, many of the *same* young men," he smirked, continuing, "Neither of us minded, and neither, it seemed, did the beautiful young Italians." For a moment, Gore

159

looked wistful. "You know Tennessee is America's top playwright. He has no peer. In the 1940s Tennessee had a very rough time. He could not get critics to review his plays because of his sexual orientation. It was unfair and demoralizing but at a certain point the material was so good; his art could no longer be ignored. I *am* glad for him. He certainly deserves the recognition and accolades but when a friend succeeds, a little something in me dies."

Jackie laughed, "You should be ashamed of yourself."

Gore laughed, "Sad, isn't it, but true!"

Jackie then remarked, "Weren't you lucky to share your 'hobby' with a friend!" She laughed and maybe because of the cocktails, confessed, "The most I can offer is, I finally lost my virginity in an elevator in Paris."

Gore's eyes lit up, he cocked his head and raised an eyebrow. "Well, well, that's quite the bombshell. Hmmm, was it everything you thought *it* would be?"

Jackie laughed, "After such a buildup, I have to say my initial thought was, 'that's it?' Back then I was seeing a young writer, or I should say, he was trying to be a writer."

"The same man that you saw when Jack sent that telegram?" Gore asked.

"Yes, that one! Back then, when I was an exchange student, we had spent the evening as we always did at a local bistro where we met friends, ate, and drank lots of table wine. Afterwards, we took a romantic walk along the Left Bank by the river."

"I can see where this is leading," Gore said smirking.

"You know how it was back then? I put him off," she shrugged with a smile, "for as long as I could but I found him overwhelmingly irresistible."

"I am well acquainted with the feeling!" Gore laughed.

Jackie continued, "We were in this rather slow and creaking elevator going up to his apartment passionately kissing. I was up against the wall grate without realizing my skirt was hiked up. Before I could stop myself, I was swept away."

"No doubt by hormones," Gore quipped.

Jackie smiled. It was finally done and at the time she was glad. Sometimes she would think about that surrendering moment in the Paris elevator, and she would experience a tummy flutter or wake up from a dream flushed. Memory can either diminish or amplify life's defining moments.

"That's quite the story. Tell me, did you have more adventures before you settled down and married at the ripe old age of what...24?"

Gore caught the waiter's eye and held up his cocktail glass signaling for another round.

"Well, besides the elevator," Jackie smiled and leaned forward with an elbow on the table and rested her chin on her hand, "There was Lee's and my Grand Tour of Europe. After her high school graduation, Lee wore our mother down to a nub begging to let us go alone. Still, we weren't allowed until Mummy and Uncle Hugh had made all these letters of introduction for us in each city."

"How was that?"

"Great, and sometimes, not so great" she shrugged. "We had to be on our best behavior. It was exhausting. I don't recall why we shared a cabin on the ship's crossing with this elderly lady, Miss Coones. I can't believe I still remember her name." Jackie laughed. "She was something like a hundred, but probably more like sixty, and scary with her clothes on."

"Oh, no don't tell me!"

"Yes, you guessed it!" Jackie laughed, "She had this annoying habit of switching the light on and off in the middle of the night. I was at my wits end when I threw back the curtain only to see this bony old woman naked without a stitch on."

"You must be positively scarred for life!"

said Gore in exaggerated horror, he splayed his fingers in front of his face.

"I don't look forward to growing old, that's for sure!" Jackie laughed.

"Does it bother you that Lee is green with envy?"

"Of what?"

"Of you, of course!" Gore said. "That little worm, Truman, let it slip."

"You are ridiculous," Jackie remarked frowning. "Truman Capote told you this?"

Gore nodded.

Then reasoning, Jackie offered, "I am four years older. I suppose a younger sister would naturally feel some competition."

"But you don't?" Gore added, "She did beat you to the altar," and waited to see the reaction.

"So?" Jackie protested. "She married in April of '53. I married in September."

"She was only what, 19? She probably married that banker, to get away from your mother," he laughed. "But you married a senator. Your wedding was touted as the wedding of the decade. Lee divorced the banker...not nearly enough cash. Capote, the blabbermouth, spilled that too. Then she married a prince. Granted a prince from a not so impressive dynasty, but still, it made her a titled princess."

"Gore, I knew you were a snob, but I don't think I appreciated to what degree."

"It is true, my wickedness and snobbery know no bounds! Of course, Stash is a dashing and cultured man," Gore added.

"He is," Jackie readily agreed feeling provoked on some level to defend her brother-in-law. "Lucky for me that Jack agrees that Stash is tremendous; because I enjoy spending so much of my time with Lee and it is fortunate for Jack that he and Stash have so much in common."

As sisters, Jackie was the older, brainy one and Lee the younger pretty sister. Jackie did not mind, but what she had resented was that she had to hide her intelligence because as her mother warned, it would intimidate prospective suitors. But when she was a Paris exchange student, this supposed "deficit" became an asset.

At Miss Porter's School for Girls in Connecticut, Jackie was always at the top of her class and was popular with the other girls. She did not have ready cash at her disposal like her wealthy classmates; her father struggled to send her a monthly allowance, but she made up for it by creating her own distinctive style. Even in Newport, at her debutante ball, where she competed with other girls her age, she chose an off-the-rack gown in direct contrast with the other girls who had dresses made just for them. It hardly mattered, her radiance and intellect shone, and she was named "Debutante of the Year." Her mother was pleased. It was all coming together. After all, Janet's girls were being bred to make good marriages to important, powerful, and hopefully wealthy men.

Jackie wanted more than that. For her, independence and an interesting life was more important; but to live the way she hoped to live, money and acquiring it, was a factor she could not afford to ignore. She was determined to find a man who interested her and stimulated her both intellectually and sexually. It would take some time, but she was not in a hurry. She would know when the right man came along.

"Weren't you engaged before you married, Jack? What happened?"

"That's simple. Quite suddenly, I realized I didn't want my mother's life. Ladies club luncheons, golf, charity work, not to mention tedious conversations with women who didn't interest me. I called it off. He was crushed. Probably more embarrassed than anything. I decided to wait and then Jack came along."

"That *was* smart!" Gore asked, "getting back to your adventure, where in Venice did you and Lee stay?"

"At the Danieli, after all, Uncle Hugh was paying, so we didn't have to rough it," she smirked. "Our room faced the Grand Canal, and we had a beautiful view of the Chiesa di San Giorgio Maggiore."

"Ah, yes, a beautiful church on a charming little island just across from that stunning hotel. I know it well. How was your Italian then?"

"It got better as the days wore on." Jackie smiled. "Come e` il tuo Italiano?"

"Meglio col passare del tempo," Gore answered her question inquiring the status of his Italian which he claimed, "Gets better as time goes on."

"Buono," Jackie laughed.

The waiter arrived with two more gin and tonics. Fortuitously, the glasses were small. Jackie picked up one of them, removed the stirrer and took a sip.

"Mmmm, delicious!" Continuing and with a broad grin, "I remember this head porter at the hotel was the most terrifying man we had ever met. He treated us like disobedient children. Every day we'd ask if we had any mail and he'd look at us as if to say, 'Who would write to the likes of you!' Lee was so incensed she convinced him she was an opera student!"

"No kidding!" Gore was amused.

Laughing, Jackie continued, "So this head porter got Lee an appointment with the queen of the sopranos. There we were at her palazzo on the Grand Canal. The palace was so intimidating, we sat shaking. The soprano was in the next room singing scales and the house shook. When she finally greeted us, Lee was so terrified she could barely speak and when Lee tried to sing, she sounded like a screeching cat being run over." Gore and Jackie laughed. "Of course, I was in hysterics. We couldn't get out of there fast enough."

Gore laughed. "I wonder if that porter recognizes you as that young guest, he was so mean to?"

"I wonder," she laughed and wrinkled her nose, "I can make Lee howl whenever I bring up that experience. During that same trip, we met the great Bernard Berenson."

"The world's leading authority on the Renaissance," Gore said confirming that he knew to whom she referred.

Jackie nodded, "He had a villa just outside Florence. Lee tried to get back at me by telling

167

Berenson I was an artist. I kicked her under the table."

Gore laughed. "Still painting?" he asked curiously.

"For my own amusement. Jack thinks my paintings are whimsical. Another way of saying, I'm not so great and not hurt my feelings."

"I don't know, your paintings have a certain, je ne sais quoi."

Jackie laughed, "Hmmm! I did one of Jack and me on the White House lawn. I captured the house perfectly got the columns straight and everything. Jack is easy to do. I just give him a blockhead, thick hair and put him in a dark suit with brown shoes to match his hair. I think brown shoes are funny, so I always have him wearing them. And I put a few dogs running on the lawn."

Gore laughed. "Frame it for Jack's office!"

Jackie laughed, "I did!"

"Berenson's most famous client was Isabella Stewart Gardner. He helped amass her art collection in Boston," Gore remarked.

"That's right. It was fascinating to hear how they conspired against the big guns when they were at art auctions. When Berenson realized their competition outbidding her was the Metropolitan Museum of Art, they worked out a system and enlisted art school students to bid for her."

"That's a pretty good plan," Gore agreed.

Jackie nodded, "I think so too. She or Berenson would signal the student to bid when a painting she wanted came up on the auction block. When the museum thought she didn't want it, they lost interest. The Metropolitan didn't catch on for quite some time."

"Intriguing, what a smart cookie."

"What a missed opportunity not asking him about Mrs. Gardner and what she was really like. I feel like a fool."

"Chalk it up to youth!" Gore offered kindly.

"I suppose," Jackie gratefully agreed and continued. "Berenson was 86 when we met him. He had a beautiful house and the way he lived surrounded by art and beauty was so wonderful. I was very impressionable. I learned the stock market isn't the *only* thing in life. The advice he gave me was to spend my time with inspiring work and life-enhancing people."

"That eliminates several people I should think," Gore quipped.

They both laughed.

"Have you been to Gardner's Venetian palace in what was considered the boonies when she built it?" Jackie added, "My God, what vision she had."

"It is a marvel," Gore said, "I love the surprise of that extraordinary indoor courtyard and the way she installed Sargent's Spanish dancer painting. It hits you right between the eyes!"

"*El Jaleo*," Jackie supplied the title. "It is a stunner. Mrs. Gardner had a fabulous eye. So wonderful that she made her house a museum."

"The super-rich who collect ultimately for the public good deserve a higher place in heaven. If such a place exists. Sargent was lucky she was his benefactor."

Pondering Berenson's advanced years, Gore changed the subject, "Life is hard, but when the time comes do you think you'll be able to let go?"

"Well, that depends upon how much life I feel I have lived," Jackie replied. "And do you feel you have lived?"

"I'm only thirty-six, so I'd have to say I'm just getting started," Gore offered, "and yet, I feel like I've had three or four lives by now."

Two women at the bar eyed Jackie. She tried not to notice.

"One of the things I love about Jack, is that he devours life, like a man sucking the meat out of a lobster claw." Without looking, she asked, "Do you think those women are lesbians?"

"Quite possibly. They do seem rather interested in you."

"Gosh," she said, bugging her eyes comically, but not particularly bothered.

Jackie continued. "Lee and I eventually presented Mummy with a journal of our European escapades. Somehow, it escaped her notice that we weren't always wearing our 'Sunday Best' like we'd promised. I remember there is a picture of me in Venice wearing short shorts and my toga sandals."

"What no gloves?" Gore teased.

"Really!" Jackie acknowledged, nodding.

"In addition to photographs that I pasted in the book, my drawings are quite hilarious. Those very dull galas provided loads of inspiration."

"Friends of Uncle Hugh, no doubt!" Gore added, chuckling at his own joke. Jackie laughed nodding.

"Lee got stuck dancing with old generals, stepping on her feet. I was luckier tripping the light fantastic with handsome young men. I don't know how I escaped dancing with the old ones."

"Just luck, I guess" Gore said, enjoying the description.

Blue Hair & Flappers

The waiter came for the dessert dishes. Gore signaled another round of gin and tonics.

"I enjoyed dinner the other night at The Compound. Security has certainly tightened up since the last time I was there."

"It is an annoying aspect, but that's life now. As you can imagine, it takes some getting used to."

Jackie pulled a cigarette from her purse; Gore lit it for her. Exhaling, she offered, "I keep my detail on their toes."

"Do you plot and scheme like a naughty schoolgirl?" Gore asked.

"Something like that. In June after the Vienna Summit, Jack had to get back to Washington, but I extended my stay. I was traveling in Greece with Lee and Stash. We had several days of swimming, and then we went to Athens to see the sights."

"You weren't bothered by the paparazzi?"

"Not at first. By the second day, after word got out, our boat was surrounded by other boats *and* the paparazzi. It was just awful. My heart sank because I thought our vacation was ruined. Then Mr. Hill got the Greek Navy to block off a swath of water so we could have some privacy."

It was quick thinking on Hill's part to enlist two American agents of Greek descent to accompany them to Greece and be part of the First Lady's detail. They came in handy when Hill used them to ask the Greek government to intervene on her behalf and call on the Greek Navy.

While they were still in Paris, Hill had mentioned to her that Ken Giannoules would assist in Greece. When they arrived in Greece, Jackie had a question about her luggage. She went up to Ken and addressed him as Mr. Giannoules, never having met him, and pronounced his name perfectly. The agent was taken aback, so much so, that he mentioned it to Hill. As Clint already knew, Jackie was surprising in so many ways.

Gore sipped some water, "Bravo, Mr. Hill! So, you were saying about Athens?"

"We drove up from our villa that was just outside Athens to have lunch with the king and queen at their palace. It wasn't far. As we were leaving, their 21-year-old son drove up in his new Mercedes convertible. I guess he was proud to show it off." She shrugged and smirked, "The prince asked me if I'd like to go for a ride?"

"And of course, you would!" Gore said, incredulously but amused.

"It was all very spontaneous."

"Undoubtedly!"

"I hopped in the car, and we sped off. When the road spread out enough, we were doing one hundred...and not kilometers," she pointed out. Jackie laughed, and briefly looked over at Mr. Hill who was watching her with a slight smile on his face. Maybe his ears were burning.

"I know it wasn't nice, but I couldn't stop laughing. We stopped briefly at the port so the prince could show me his sailboat."

"That's not a euphemism, is it?" Gore said kidding, his mind as usual preoccupied with sexual proclivity.

"Stop!" Jackie shook her head, smirking.

"Afterwards the prince drove me back to my villa. The other car came to a screeching halt. There was a lot of screaming and yelling at the prince... not at me." Adding, "It's a ride I won't forget!" She laughed.

"And neither will Mr. Hill, I'd guess. You could have caused an international incident!" Gore laughed shaking his head.

"I don't suppose I thought much about it then or since," She responded, frankly.

"Think of it, if his car sailed off a cliff or flipped over with you in it, it would have caused an international incident," Gore reasoned.

Jackie shrugged, "Yes, I suppose so, but I take the blame."

"If only life were *that* simple," Gore mused.

Mr. Hill had not planned it this way but because she trusted him more than other agents and because he was more flexible than his boss who was initially in charge; by summer of the first year, he became head of her detail. Jackie abhorred the paparazzi, and he understood why as they were relentless in their pursuit of her. Still, both he and Jackie were grateful for one moment captured when a photographer snapped a picture of them in Italy in an overcrowded rowboat that was practically sinking. Hill was shouting frantically at onlookers to put down their cameras and give them a push, the boat was at the near point of flooding or tipping over. In the photograph, Jackie is in hysterics laughing. Her teasing he could take. He bonded to her more than he could have predicted.

"Life is more than schedules," she added picking up the fresh cocktail. With a bit of irony asked, "Is your intention to get me bombed? I didn't notice you asking for these!"

"Don't be silly, we've been sitting here nearly three hours, I know you can handle a few drinks. Are you feeling tipsy?"

"A bit. Worst case, I'll have you and Mr. Hill on either side of me and my feet will barely touch the sidewalk." They both laughed.

"You realize with Jack in office, you two have awakened the country from what seemed a deep sleep."

Jackie mused, "The Country, Sleeping Beauty, what a metaphor!"

"I'm serious!" Gore protested.

Jackie nodded acquiescingly, "I suppose so after the Eisenhowers. They seemed older than their ages. The world does seem open to us." Then thinking about it added, "And to you, too. You seem to know everybody!"

"I suppose that is true. Some so old, and by now, so obscure, they need a footnote!" He laughed. "Who even *knows* who Mona Bismarck is?"

"I don't." Jackie questioned, "Something tells me I *should*?"

"Mona, *you should know,* was one of the first

women on the *Best Dressed List*, a place she occupied for decades, and the first woman to dye her white hair blue. Surprisingly, it worked for her. Salvador Dali even painted her with her blue hair. It could be the reason he painted her."

"I am amazed I've never heard of her."

"Well even to me it seems another lifetime ago. Almost like it happened to someone else. Mona was friends with the Duke and Duchess of Windsor."

"Those two, I *do* know!" Jackie interjected.

"Yes," Gore nodded, "A hundred years ago, I spent two Christmas Eves with Mona and *them!* England was lucky the duke abdicated the throne for Wallis. *That* American divorcee had a flapper's wise-cracking charm," Gore quipped, "I rather liked her."

On a roll, Gore added, "There is an adage, 'When you marry for money you earn every penny.' This had to be true in Wallis's case. The duke always had something of such riveting stupidity to say on any subject, that I clung to his every word."

"Gosh! Don't let *me* get on your bad side!"

"Not a chance!" Gore laughed. "As a writer, I've been lucky to know other writers...some of them with real merit." Gore could be snarky. "In the early days, I was introduced to my good friend, Christopher Isherwood. He introduced me to W.H. Auden, Evelyn Waugh, and E.M. Forster, to whom I took an instant dislike. It's hard to believe Forster was capable of such beautiful novels as *A Room with a View* and *A Passage to India*."

"I loved both those wonderful books. Don't spoil them for me."

"I'll try not to," Gore acknowledged. "The war was over, of course. We laughed a great deal in those circles. But to an American eye, English life was a terrible, rationed drabness." Gore paused then asked, "Do you mind if I have one of your cigarettes?"

"I didn't think you smoked?" Jackie said reaching in her bag. She handed Gore the pack, he slipped one out for each of them. Lighting both, he handed Jackie hers and dragged on his.

Exhaling, Gore said, "I always knew I wanted to write but those early novels didn't exactly make me rich. That's why I went to Hollywood to write screenplays and then to New York to write television scripts. I have met a lot of interesting people. After a while, you get to know who is real and who are the fakers."

"You know Paul Newman and Joanne Woodward," Jackie remarked.

"I do. They are real, not fakers. It may

interest you to know, Joanne and I dated for a year...before Paul, of course. We pretended to be engaged when our grandmothers visited me at my house on the Hudson." Gore took a long drag, looked Jackie in the eye, and exhaled, "I'm not *adverse* to women, I just prefer men."

Jackie bit her index finger, "Maybe, I'm *not* as safe as I imagined." Gore laughed.

Gore adored his house on the Hudson River. It was his first real home. When he bought it in 1950, he could barely afford it, let alone furnish it. Edgewater, as it was called, was set near railroad tracks, an aspect of the house he was unaware of when he bought it. What a shock it was the first night he stayed there when the train came roaring by. The house shook and the train's warning whistle made itself known, in no uncertain terms, just how close the train was. After a while, Gore barely noticed the train or its scheduled passings. However, the train still had the capability to unnerve any guests who visited.

"So, what are the Newmans really like?" Jackie asked, straightening in her chair, then leaning in, an elbow on the table and her chin resting in her hand. "Tell me everything!"

"Fun," Gore said enjoying the cigarette,

twirling it in his fingers. "We shared a house in Malibu that was filled with people on the weekends. I thought they were Paul and Joanne's friends. They thought they were my friends. It was a wild and interesting time...another world. It seems like a parallel universe now."

"Yes," Jackie agreed, "I can see that."

"When we met, Paul was a star, Joanne, not as well-known, was an actress. Paul became an actor later."

"He's an incredibly good-looking man."

"Yes, tell me about it!" His eyes widened, "I was in Paris with them last year. Paul was doing a film with Sophia Loren. Joanne rented this cold horrible apartment because she thought it would be romantic. It was just cold. Fortunately, I stayed in a hotel. We both kept asking Paul, what's Sophia like? He was very closed mouth about her. He'd answer things like; she was punctual, or she knows her lines. It was maddening. Naturally, Joanne was imagining the worst." He finished with, "It may interest you to know they are Democrats."

"Well, Jack cares about that. I am interested in politics for what can be done for humanity. It sounds lofty but I really mean it. I spent time talking with coalminers' wives in their shacks during Jack's campaigning and there are some experiences that never leave you."

"I know what you mean, I have seen that kind of poverty too," Gore agreed.

It was almost ironic to think that Jackie had not been considered an asset but instead a liability back in the early days of Jack's bid for the presidency. Most of the people in charge of his campaign thought that Jackie's refinement, the way she spoke, the way she dressed would be alien to average Americans and they not accepting her would hurt Jack's chances. The one person who was firmly in her camp was Jack's father. He thought she could be an asset that could add polish, if not pizazz on the trail, which could be monotonous and dull even for the candidates. As it turned out, Joe had been right all along. Not only did the public, and especially women, accept her, they went crazy for her and tried to emulate her in every way possible.

"Living in the White House has the advantage of being able to meet anyone. We had Greta Garbo to dinner. Jack gave her a piece of scrimshaw."

Nodding, Gore said, "Garbo said the president gave her a piece of scrimshaw. She also told me that you said to her, 'Jack never gave me a whale's tooth.' You should know Garbo got a big kick out of that."

Jackie smiled, her eyes shining.

"Howard and I stayed with her in Switzerland. But I keep an eye on her... she steals my clothes."

Jackie seemed genuinely surprised, not about the clothing theft but that Garbo and Gore were friends. "Really? But, of course, you know Greta Garbo, you really do know everyone!"

"That famous quote, 'I want to be alone,' is a misquote. What she really said was; 'I want to be *left* alone.' Two entirely different meanings."

"Quite."

"After the Army, I was going to run for the Senate. But then, I ended up in New York working for Dutton Publishing. Dutton printed my first book. I thought I had some sway with them. I tried to get them to publish, *Go Tell It on the Mountain*, by James Baldwin whom I'd met in Rome at a party. The same party where I met Tennessee. Baldwin is a vivid individual full of energy. His personality oscillates between Martin Luther King Jr. and Bette Davis." Gore laughed. "But Dutton would not do it. The owner was from Virginia; that was his excuse for not publishing Baldwin."

Jackie thought back to her school days in Connecticut at the prestigious Miss Porter's when she was in her private high school. It was the 1940s, well before the *Brown v. The Board of Education* Supreme Court case that challenged segregation and discrimination in public schools. At the time, she had chafed at the exclusively white student body and questioned why there were no scholarships for girls of more diverse backgrounds. She just did not think it was fair. Jackie's sense of fairness, compared with society's lack of it, was enlightened, especially given her privileged background.

Jackie shook her head at that, "Jack hopes to make a difference for all Americans. Big changes are long overdue."

"We're all looking forward to that! I'll settle the bill. We should dash for the theater. It isn't far."

Gore raised his arm and signaled the waiter.

Queen of Sheba

When they came out into the street, the sun was lower, the buildings had an orange glow. Up ahead, there was an ice cream stand. "Let's get a cone," she requested.

"Let me get them. Go look at the water with Clint and I'll bring them. What kind?"

"Vanilla...or pistachio if they have it."

Gore got three vanilla cones, carried them precariously and handed one to each of them. "Mr. Hill doesn't usually eat on the job," Jackie said laughing and added, "I can manage my cone and walking if you two can."

With that, the three kept moving. They reached the theater which was located on the water side at St. Mary's of the Harbor church just a few blocks away. The theater was not in the church itself but in the building next to it that had been converted into a playhouse. Gore produced three tickets and handed them to the ticket taker. The usher gave a program to Gore and Clint, and when he suddenly recognized Jackie, he handed her the entire stack.

Jackie smiled, took one and gave back the rest.

The seats were unassigned. She lowered her eyes and found two empty places on one of the long benches for Gore and herself. Clint took a place behind them with a satisfiable vantage point and not for viewing the play. He was discreet but his eyes were everywhere.

The playhouse filled in rapidly until nearly every seat was taken. There was a buzz in the room as people began to suspect just who was in their midst. Jackie had an aisle seat discreetly near the wall, clear of any other person. There was room to slip out of the theater if the situation became unruly. So far, the theater goers were playing it cool.

Gore sat beside Jackie and engaged her in conversation. She rested a hand on her face to obscure it. She did not make eye contact with anyone. The lights went down, and the play started. In 1905 *Mrs. Warren's Profession* was performed on the London stage. Back then, when the play finished and the curtain came down, the cast was subsequently arrested for obscenity because the subject matter was deemed scandalous. It took a while for the plot to thicken. The audience was not exactly on the edge of their seats. Times had changed and the impact in 1961 was considerably less than it had been in 1905.

At the play's conclusion, the curtain came down and went up again. The actors came forward and took their bows. The house lights were about to come up when Clint gave Gore a signal that the time was right to slip out. Clint was directly behind them when they made their way out to the street. A crowd had gathered outside. Word had spread.

Jackie knew what to do. She lowered her head not making eye contact with anyone save for Gore. She grabbed him by the arm and pulled herself close. Mr. Hill stepped into action pulling in front of her and cleared a path. "Please let us through," became his mantra.

"I know of a place not far from here," Gore offered.

"Lead the way," Jackie said, determined not to be deterred.

She was not willing to give up on the evening just yet. They walked swiftly. It was darkish on Commercial Street. The shops were closed and after hours, only a few had illuminated windows. The streetlights were dim and that worked in their favor. Gore recognized the establishment he was looking for, a house really, with a small sign that read, 'Ace of Spades.'

The door did not open so he rang the bell. A man opened the door halfway.

"Can I help you?"

"Yes, we were hoping for a nightcap," Gore answered.

"Are you members?" asked the man.

"Well, no we aren't but I'm sure you'll want to make an exception," Gore offered brightly.

Jackie raised her gaze and smiled at the doorman.

"You got I.D.?" asked the man rather gruffly.

"You don't know who I am?" Jackie asked.

Clint held back patiently but he was not liking this situation one bit.

Gore almost laughed, "Surely this woman needs no introduction!"

"I don't care if she's the Queen of Sheba, no identification, no admission. Rules are rules." With that, he abruptly closed the door.

Gore looked at Jackie and she at him and they both burst into laughter. "Anymore bright ideas?" Jackie shrugged still laughing.

"I know just the place," Gore answered, regretting that he had not thought of it before.

Gore took them down a side street. There was a bar at the end that he had been to previously.

The door opened easily, and Clint pushed apart heavy drapes and scanned the room. He fleetingly thought to himself that he hoped they would not later find themselves the subjects of a raid. He imagined his boss would have his head on a platter, and he could not begin to think of the President's reaction if they were arrested. His argument that his job description was to allow the First Lady to do the things she most wanted and keep her safe was not about to hold water in such a circumstance.

Jackie and Gore made their way down the steps. Clint took a bar stool on the left side of the bar, Gore and Jackie took seats in the center. Music by Dave Brubeck played. The place had a nice vibe. Jackie began to relax. The street crowd had unnerved her but only slightly. The bar was an intimate space and dimly lit which she appreciated. She noticed behind the bar, two ginger jar lamps with fringed shades. On the wall above each lamp hung a large black and white framed poster; one was Marlon Brando from *A Streetcar Named Desire* looking buff and masculine in a torn tee-shirt and the other of glamorous Marlene Dietrich from *Morocco* wearing a man's tailored tuxedo.

The bar itself had lighted shelves that featured the liquor bottles to best advantage. The array of different types of glassware signaled that your cocktail would be served in the appropriate glass. A handsome barman, wearing fitted jeans and a fitted black tee-shirt, motorcycle boots, and a red bandanna artfully shoved in his back pocket, stood behind the bar off to the side wiping glasses with a dry cloth. His muscled arms had just the right amount of body hair. His only adornments were a large-faced watch with a three-inch leather strap and an over-sized silver skull ring. When Jackie imagined a night cap in Provincetown, this bar was exactly what she pictured. The barman approached Gore and Jackie with a nod.

"Evening," said Gore pleasantly, "Two Cognacs, please."

Jackie reached into her bag and found her cigarettes. She pulled one out and held it between her lips resting the cigarette on two fingers that formed a V. Gore lit it for her. She exhaled, directing the smoke toward the ceiling and crossed her legs. The barman served them. They raised glasses and sipped. Clint, approached by the barman, asked for a Coke. He kept an eye on the entrance and the customers.

"Well, how did you enjoy the play?" Gore asked.

Exhaling, "Actually, my favorite part was when the usher recognized us and got so discombobulated, he handed me all the programs."

Gore laughed and nodded, "That *was* good!"

"Word certainly traveled," she said, swirling her Cognac in its snifter and sipping her drink.

"That was quite a mob outside the theater. Good thing Mr. Hill knows his way around a crowd," Gore said, impressed with how quickly they were able to contain the situation and get away.

"He has literally pulled me out of some tight spots. The crowds can sometimes be quite scary. Shopping on Fifth Avenue is over for me at this point," Jackie said, not hiding her disappointment.

"I can see why! It would be impossible unless you had the stores closed like the queen does when she feels the need to have a look around."

"Really, she does that?"

"Once in a great while, I've read. She's not the type that likes to make a fuss," Gore answered.

"I used to resent the Secret Service always having to be around constantly during our waking hours. Then Caroline almost drowned in a friend's pool. After that, I became more grateful and less resentful."

"I should think that would do it!" Gore agreed amicably. "I have to say I am stunned that we were barred from The Ace of Spades. I had no idea that it's a private club in of all places, Provincetown!"

"It's a first for me. I can tell you that," Jackie

said amused more than anything.

"I imagine it is," Gore laughed, "Heads will roll tomorrow when word gets out that the First Lady was turned away!"

Laughing Jackie added, "Not my finest moment. Whatever got into me? If you dare tell Jack I pulled rank and said, 'Do you have any idea who I am?' I promise I'll throttle you!"

Gore laughed, reliving the moment. "Wait, wait!" He gestured 'stop' with his hand. "You'll be relieved to realize it was me who pulled rank, not you. You did puff up your chest when I told the bouncer that he'd be sorry tomorrow as you were no ordinary lady."

"Well, then okay, that's a story that will certainly amuse Jack." Jackie laughed. "Permission to tell all."

Just then, the barman stopped pretending he was not listening and put down the glass he was wiping dry. "Did I hear you say you weren't allowed in the Ace of Spades?"

"That's right. Can you believe it?" Gore asked rather incredulously.

"What you didn't understand, is that it's a private club," explained the barman.

"We found that out. But still, I find it curious that we weren't allowed in. Is it possible that the bouncer didn't recognize at least one of us?" Gore asked candidly.

Keeping her cool, Jackie observed, but did not add anything to the conversation. She rested one arm around her middle grabbing hold lightly her own waist. The other arm bent keeping her cigarette elevated. She shifted and crossed her legs sitting erect.

"Hard to say," shrugged the barman. "The Ace of Spades has been around for ten years or so. It's a women's bar. They are strict about the 'membership only.' You found that out. In '52 three selectmen in town tried to shut it down. Claimed it had immoral tones. You get what I mean?"

"Sure," Gore nodded knowingly, "I get it."

"Not everyone in town agreed with the selectmen. The town had a meeting. A compromise was set. Ace could stay open if they ran it as a private club." The bartender placed both hands on the counter and added, "It's amazing to me that it is still running that way. Mainly because if you go, not only do you have to show I.D. you also have to sign in with a full name and address."

"Even now?" Gore was more than surprised.

"Yup, that's right."

"Those women are braver than most men I know." Gore turned to Jackie and explained,

"Consequences could be severe. You risk being fired if your boss found out and was vindictive, and you could be thrown out of your apartment if a landlord was so inclined. It's happened to many without recourse. It would mean disaster, if a newspaper got hold of the list and decided to print it. Incredible as it is to me, there are no laws to protect homosexuals. The cops can and have arrested women wearing pants with a front fly. Your life could be ruined."

Jackie listened but did not add anything. She sipped her Cognac watching the barman.

Addressing the barman, "I suppose men are not welcome?" Gore asked curiously.

"Not sure. I never tried to go myself."

Suddenly, Jackie spoke, "I forgot my I.D. but had the good sense to wear Capris with a side zipper!"

Gore, Jackie, and the barman laughed.

This information was new to Jackie. Like many Americans, she was unaware that this segment of the population was so at risk, so without protection. It was also a time of blatant prejudices and misunderstandings.

Even the medical profession at the time thought of homosexuality as a mental disorder. An opinion Gore never accepted or bought into.

"Well, it's their loss," offered the barman, "I'm glad to have this opportunity to meet you."

Gore and Jackie both nodded. "By the way, what's your name?" Gore asked, not without a twinkle in his eye.

The barman smiled, "Chet. Chet Barnaby."

"Well, Chet Barnaby, I'm Gore and it's a pleasure to meet you," Gore raised his glass and nodded. "From where is it that you hail?"

"Pittsburgh." Came the answer.

Gore smiled and nodded. "And when the season is over do you go back to Pittsburgh?"

"Gosh, no. Have you *been* to Pittsburgh?" Chet laughed and shook his head. "I'm off to Key West for the winter. I have another bartending gig. I'll be back here next spring."

"Well, well, you're living the good life," said Gore.

Chet returned the smiled, "So far so good. Can I get you something else?"

"No. I don't think so," Jackie smiled.

The barman returned the smile, nodded, and stepped back returning his attention to other customers. Jackie and Gore drained their glasses. Gore settled the tab and explained that he was also paying for the Coke.

"I'm planning to be at Race Point tomorrow

afternoon, any chance I'll see you there?" Gore asked hopefully.

Chet put the money in the cash register, turned around, and answered, "It's possible."

Gore got down from his bar stool first and gave Jackie his hand. She swung around and easily made a graceful descent. Gore placed a five-dollar tip on the bar and gave a final wave to the barman.

"Hope to see you at the beach. Good night, now."

The three exited the bar. Outside, Jackie smiled at Gore. "Tomorrow seems to be shaping up for you."

Gore with a glint in his eye, a smirk on his face and with hands in his pockets remarked, "Yes," as they walked up the side street back toward Commercial.

Tomorrow

Once they were on Commercial Street, "It's this way back to the car," Gore gently directed. The three of them strolled back the way they had come. Jackie taking Gore's arm and Clint Hill walking behind, close but not too close. The ocean breeze felt like a caress, salty and moist. The navy-blue sky was a blanket of clearly visible stars. Jackie recognized both the Big and Little Dipper and Hercules. It was a beautiful night.

After clearing the center of town, the street was deserted. She felt grateful for anonymity. She loved her life, but she was not unaware of the price she was paying. Life had its rewards and its penalties. She chose to look on the bright side. She felt the luckiest woman in the world.

The street was dimly lit with streetlights placed intermittently. Commercial Street angled left and continued along the water. As they neared The Moors Motel, Jackie continued to hold Gore's arm, particularly, as they made their way when the sidewalks stopped.

Bordering along the road as they walked in

near darkness, they again passed the wild grasses, dusty miller, and wild beach roses. The sandy soil spilled out onto the asphalt and was slippery in patches especially now that it was not so easy to see. Clint Hill, taking up the rear, was on lookout for oncoming cars but luckily none approached. Still, he was at the ready to shield her from any danger.

Finally, on The Moors property, they stood outside by the car.

"When do you leave the Cape?" Gore asked.

"Labor Day or thereabouts," Jackie said.

"Same here." Gore agreed.

"Where has the time gone?" Jackie asked, more of a declaration than a question. "This really has been fun," she touched his arm, "and quite the education." They both laughed.

"I can't thank you enough."

"Nonsense. I'm glad you came," Gore said.

Saying goodbye, Jackie embraced Gore with a firm hug. Gore extended his hand to Clint and he and Clint shook hands. With that Gore opened the front passenger door. Jackie slipped in. Gore shut the door. As Clint got into the driver's seat, Jackie rolled down the window all the way.

Gore bent down and put his face in the window. "Mr. Hill, take care of The Queen of Sheba for us, won't you?"

Clint and Jackie laughed.

"Of course, Mr. Vidal, you know I will. I'd do anything for Mrs. Kennedy." Clint smiled.

"Clint, when you pull out be sure to turn right and exit town using Bradford."

Clint shook his head affirmatively and said, "Thanks! And I very much appreciate you paying for the dinner, Mr. Vidal."

Gore nodded and smiled, pulled back and waved. "I'll call you, Jackie."

"Ciao," Jackie smiled and gave Gore a backwards wave popular with Italians, opening and closing her palm twice toward herself.

Hill started the engine, put the car into reverse and pulled out of the space. Jackie waved with the sweep on her hand one last time as they drove out of the motel driveway. They turned right onto Bradford Street and continued out of town in pitch darkness, the way illuminated only by their own headlights until they joined the highway to Hyannis Port.

Jackie leaned against the seat and crossed her legs. Her left hand was on the seat and her right arm draped across her lap. It was nearly midnight, but she did not feel tired.

Tomorrow would be Friday and Jack would be arriving by helicopter in the afternoon.

Author's Note

It was my friend, Peter Clemons, who brought the Provincetown newspaper clipping, a tiny paragraph in a retrospective piece, to my attention that the writer, Gore Vidal, had asked his friend, Jackie Kennedy to join him in Provincetown in August of 1961. It was an intriguing discovery and a compelling idea to write about their day together. A day that really happened but is written fictitiously from my imagination.

How amazing to be a fly on the wall to see and hear how that day unfolded. In Fred Kaplan's *Gore Vidal, A Biography* (Doubleday, 1996), it mentions how Jackie bounces on Gore's motel room bed that day in Provincetown. It is a small detail but one that gives insight into how free she must have felt about the day and spending time with him.

I was ten years old when JFK was assassinated, an event from my childhood that I never quite got over. I can still be moved to tears remembering. Many who lived during that time in history feel the same. As an adult, I read many biographies on Jackie Bouvier Kennedy Onassis and read most of Gore Vidal's novels and essays, including both of his autobiographies, *Palimpsest* (Penguin Books, 1995) and *Point to Point Navigation: A Memoir* (Doubleday, 2006). In youth, I was glued to television and witnessed Gore Vidal in action on countless television talk shows where he was in command and in high demand for more than thirty years.

Jackie was more elusive. She did not seek the limelight; it searched for her, relentlessly, mercilessly. Still, she carved out as normal a life for herself as she could, being who she was.

I came to know Clint Hill as the faithful special agent who heroically climbed onto the back of the President's car on that fateful day of the assassination and pushed Jackie back into the car, covering both her and JFK with his own body. His book, *Mrs. Kennedy and Me* by Clint Hill (Gallery Books, 2012) is a tribute to her and gave me more insight into her than many of the other books I have read through the years. I looked to it for invaluable research. Because of Clint Hill's special relationship with Jackie, in the story, I chose him as the person to drive her to Provincetown. It was another of her friends who in fact drove her, but I used artistic license here as a vehicle to give more background information on my characters and to show how contrasting backgrounds played out in their relationship.

When we see Jackie through Clint's eyes, it helps form a more dimensional portrait of her. At least, I hope that it does.

Having spent more than thirty summers myself enjoying the delights of Provincetown, I was able to describe it from personal experience. It is a beautiful vacation spot, still very much an art colony, a welcoming gay hotspot, and a wonderful place to live if you do not mind the population swelling tenfold in the summer.

I grew up in the working-class city of Woburn, ten miles outside of Boston, and as a teenager, I yearned for the urbane sophistication I saw in both my titular subjects. I admired Jackie above all else, for her resilience, style, intellect, taste, and for the way she raised and was devoted to her children. I admired Gore for his quick wit, his ability to slay his opponents in debate, his viewpoint on America and her politics, society, and shortcomings. Most of all, I admired how the only opinion he truly cared about was his own. It was a thrill once hearing him give a speech speaking out publicly for free speech at the Arlington Street Church in Boston.

When I determined to write about Jackie Kennedy, Gore Vidal, and Clint Hill, I knew I would need inspiration to interweave real information with the fiction of their conversations. I got that inspiration from several books, most notably by reading *Gore Vidal, a Biography* by Fred Kaplan (Doubleday, 1999), *All Too Human, The Love Story of Jack and Jackie Kennedy* by Edward Klein (Pocket Books, 1996), *The Kennedy White House* by Carl Sferrazza Anthony (Touchstone, 2001), *Jackie and Cassini, A Fashion Love Affair* by Lauren Marino (Running Press Adult, 2016), *One Special Summer* by Jacqueline and Lee Bouvier (Barnes Press, 1974), *Jacqueline Kennedy: The White House Years*, a compilation of material from the John F. Kennedy Library by Hamish Bowles (Bullfinch Press, 2001), *Mrs. Kennedy and Me* by Clint Hill (Gallery Books, 2012), *Upstairs at the White House: My Life with the First Ladies* by J.B. West (Open Road Media, 2016), *Capote* by Gerald Clark, (Simon & Schuster, 1988) *The Power of Style* by Annette Tapert and Diana Edkins (Random House, Inc., 1994), as well as information gleaned from various articles.

All the conversations in the book are imagined. For a time, Gore Vidal did enjoy a special relationship with JFK and Jackie, but then he had a falling out with them because of an article he wrote about JFK's brother, Bobby that was published in *Esquire Magazine* in March of 1963. As what often happens in life happened here, the rift was never repaired, and Gore became bitter.

I imagined Jackie in her bedroom, her morning, her interaction with her young children, what life was like for her in summer, her drive to Provincetown and the day she spent with Gore. I took great pleasure in concocting all of it. As characters, they were all such fun to reimagine. And in so far as I know, no one ever referred to Jackie as The Queen of Sheba, at least, not to her face.

Acknowledgements

The first person I want to thank is Peter Clemons who sent me the *Provincetown Advocate* newspaper clipping and encouraged me to write about it. Peter and I collaborated on a four-act play that I wrote with the same theme but not the same title. The play has been published but never performed. Peter was tireless in his encouragement, and I thank him for his efforts, friendship, and kindness.

Richard Stimpson read early drafts, of both the play and the book, gave me valuable advice and constructive criticism. He encouraged me to paint the scenes of people, places, and things with vivid descriptions. Deb Levene championed and encouraged me after reading countless early drafts. Deb, who has known me for decades, understood what I was trying to create and teased out more depth than I knew I was capable. Our long-detailed conversations helped bring the work into sharper perspective and shape. Renée Beltrand edited the first drafts. No small task. She caught details that I missed and did more to boost the project than she knows.

I would also like to express appreciation to Esther Griswold, Christel Antonellis, and other friends and family who agreed to read drafts and gave encouragement. I especially would like to thank Ellen Fiascone for her thoughtful comments, the late Douglas Sulzer, Susan Bergeron-West and the late Dana Faris for volunteering editing expertise. Dana Faris was an invaluable resource and a wealth of knowledge.

To literary agent, Colleen Mohyde who read drafts, acted as a sounding board, and offered advice, I extend to you my warmest appreciation.

Thank you to Steve Tringali for giving moral support and the use of your printer and to Jo Tringale, my mother-in-law, a woman of style herself, and a big admirer of Jackie. Jo, now at age 94, read both drafts of the play and the book and buoyed me with her enthusiasm for the project.

And finally, a tremendous thank you to Kevin Tringale, my husband of more than 40 years, whom, when introducing him, I jokingly refer to as my "first husband." The most important decision one makes in life, is choosing the right person to spend your life. For me Kevin is that person. We have traveled the world together and we still have fun. Kevin read every draft, and there were many, made important suggestions and edited what was the 'final' draft many times. I thank him for his love, kindness and for understanding how much this project has meant to me.